Praise for K(
One Wicked Night

"*One Wicked Night* was a great read...I enjoyed the twists and turns in the story...emotions and feelings are fully engaged the entire time."

~ *Night Owl Reviews*

"*One Wicked Night* needs an additional disclaimer...have some tissues handy. While I love Kelly Jamieson's books and they way that she depicts her characters, I never expected *One Wicked Night* to be a tear jerker. I can honestly say that I don't think *One Wicked Night* will be a story that is easily forgotten..."

~ *Sizzling Hot Book Reviews*

"Gripping story...keeps you captivated. Fantastic read."

~ *Sensual Reads*

"...an amazing story that is both moving and incredibly sexy at the same time. You can't help but fall in love with Kaelin, Nick and Tyler..."

~ *Guilty Pleasures Book Reviews*

10 12

Look for these titles by
Kelly Jamieson

Now Available:

Love Me

Friends With Benefits

Love Me More

2 Hot 2 Handle

Lost and Found

Rule of Three

Sweet Deal

Hot Ride

Print Anthology

Love 2 Love U

One Wicked Night

Kelly Jamieson

SAMHAIN
PUBLISHING

Samhain Publishing, Ltd.
11821 Mason Montgomery Road, 4B
Cincinnati, OH 45249
www.samhainpublishing.com

Editing by Sue Ellen Gower
Cover by Scott Carpenter

First Samhain Publishing, Ltd. electronic publication: October 2011
First Samhain Publishing, Ltd. print publication: September 2012

Dedication

There are so many people I have to thank for helping with this book: my wonderful critique partner Nara Malone for her valuable feedback; all of the Nine Naughty Novelists for their incredible friendship, support and encouragement through challenging times, in particular, PG Forte and Erin Nicholas who read this manuscript and also gave feedback; as always my family who support me no matter what; and most especially goddess editor Sue-Ellen Gower—thank you from the bottom of my heart for your support and input! I'm so glad we're working together again, Suz!

Chapter One

The last time Kaelin Daume had seen Tyler Wirth and Nick Kernsted, they'd been naked, and they'd had a naked girl tied to a chair.

The memory of that had been seared into Kaelin's brain, haunting her more times than she wanted to admit. In fact, every time she had sex she thought about it. Which could be one reason her sex life wasn't all that great.

She swallowed hard as she tugged the plastic garment bag down over the bridesmaid dress in her bedroom. Now that she was about to see Tyler and Nick again, nerves jumped in her stomach. She took a breath. She had no choice. She had to do this. She picked up the dress and her purse, slid her feet into a pair of sandals and headed for her back door.

She passed the living room where Taz lay on the couch, nose between his paws, giving her the sad puppy dog eyes he did every time she went out. "I won't be late," she said to him as if he understood. "You'll be fine."

He didn't lift his nose, but when she backed her car out of the short driveway, his little black-and-white face appeared in the window from his perch on the back of the couch, his favorite place to sit and watch the world go by. The way he watched her leave, head tilted sadly to one side, tugged at her heart, as always. She was way too softhearted about him. "I wish I was staying home with you," she muttered, even though she was in the car and this time there was no hope of Taz hearing, let alone understanding.

Margot Wirth sat in front of the computer in her office. Or what they called her office. Not that she'd ever had any business to conduct there, other than household business such as paying bills and online shopping. She rolled her chair in closer and clicked on her email program. Yes. There was a message from him.

Warmth spread through her as she read his email, chatty and warm and funny, and she smiled as she started tapping in her reply. Then her husband spoke from behind her.

"What are you doing? People are going to be here any minute."

She started and quickly minimized the program, then turned to smile at Ken. At sixty he was still attractive, his dark hair now mostly gray and receding just slightly, but still thick. His athletic body had softened a little, but he was still in good shape even though he did little to stay that way. Unlike she, who worked out every other day, played tennis and golf in the summer and ran on the indoor track at the gym in the winter. And she was ten years younger than he.

"I know," she said. "Just had one more little thing to do for the dinner tomorrow night." Their daughter's wedding had been a welcome diversion in her mind-numbing life of shopping, decorating, golf and gossip at the Mapleglen Country Club.

"I thought Tyler would be here by now."

"Should be any time now. They're driving down from Chicago."

Nerves fluttered in her stomach. They hadn't seen their son for nearly ten years, after that horrific incident with the Brown family. But Avery had insisted that her little brother be there for her wedding and had somehow convinced him to come home. And had also convinced her father Tyler should be there.

Margot longed to see both her children with a deep, aching yearning, especially Tyler. She'd never been able to get over losing him like that, had never told her husband about her efforts to keep track of him, to make sure he was okay, to know how he was doing. She knew her hopes for this wedding were silly and unreasonable, but god, would they ever have another chance to rebuild their family? For her to see her two children together, as adults, to see her daughter begin her married life, to see the man Tyler had become. In some ways she was nervous, terrified that he was not going to live up to her husband's impossible expectations. Because she'd come to realize that her own impossible expectations were just that...impossible. On the other hand, she knew enough about Tyler that she was also filled with excited anticipation and maternal pride.

"God, I'll be glad when this wedding is over," Ken said.

She pressed her lips together. When this was over... She closed her eyes. When this was over her life would go back to normal. And she wasn't sure if she could stand it.

Kaelin paused at the front door of the Wirth home, the location of that erotic, disturbing scene she'd accidentally witnessed ten years earlier, and forced herself to ring the doorbell, palms sweating. Then the door opened and Mrs. Wirth stood there. "Hello, Kaelin! Come in."

Kaelin smiled at her best friend's mom, so pretty with her

shoulder-length blonde hair and slender figure. As usual she looked impeccable in a sleeveless flowered silk dress but Kaelin, despite being so nervous herself, didn't miss the tightness at the corners of Mrs. Wirth's eyes or the tension in her smile.

This family wedding might kill them all before it was done.

As she stepped into the foyer, Tyler was the next person she saw through the open French doors into the living room, and the sight of him made her stomach drop and her pulse leap.

"Kaelin!" Her best friend Avery Wirth hurtled from the living room of the big old two-story Victorian house belonging to her parents. "You're here!"

Kaelin dragged her eyes away from Tyler, stunningly gorgeous, still magnetically attractive, who'd turned to look at her when his sister Avery called her name. She focused on her best friend who she hadn't seen in months, excruciatingly aware of Tyler in her peripheral vision.

"I'm here." She smiled and lifted her arms. "With the dress."

Avery took the dress and hung it on a coat tree then they hugged in a long, tight embrace. "So good to see you," Avery murmured.

"You too," Kaelin said and they drew back to smile at each other.

Avery took her arm and led her into the living room. "Come say hi," she said. "Tyler and Nick are here, and my mom and dad, and you can meet Scott's parents too."

The Wirth family was gathering for Avery's wedding the coming weekend, reunited in Mapleglen, Illinois, where Kaelin and Avery had grown up together, best friends since middle school.

Kaelin hugged Scott, Avery's fiancé, who she'd met a handful of times. Avery had met Scott in Los Angeles, where she now lived. Kaelin approved of him as a husband for her best friend. Tall and lean, with a slightly receding hairline that did nothing to diminish his good looks, he handled Avery's energetic personality perfectly. Kaelin shook hands with Scott's parents when he introduced her, hugged Avery's father, Dr. Wirth, and then she was face-to-face with Tyler.

Her cheeks heated and her stomach tightened, but she smiled politely as she greeted him. God, she'd never thought the next time she saw him would be in a room full of people, but maybe that was better. A rush of emotions flooded her—remembered shock, heartbreak, disappointment and...arousal.

"Hey, Kaelin." He took her hand in his, big and warm. Lord, Avery's little brother had grown up, way up, a good eight inches taller than her five foot six, and he'd grown out too, sporting a pair of shoulders that would do a football player proud, though he was still long and lean. "Long time no see."

"It has been a while," she choked out. His face was inscrutable, his mouth firm, his cobalt-blue eyes cool and unreadable. As a teenager, Tyler had been good-looking in a sexy, wicked way. Ten years ago, he'd worn his dark gold hair long and straight. Now it was cut shorter, with a casual messy look and sideburns. His lean jaw and chin with its deep cleft wore a heavy layer of dark gold stubble that only added to the wicked charm.

"You remember Nick?"

She turned her attention to Tyler's friend Nick, pulling her hand back from Tyler's grip, resisting the urge to yank it free.

Did she remember Nick? Of course she remembered him. The emails they'd exchanged over the years from time to time had ensured that. But Tyler didn't know about that.

"Of course." She smiled at Nick.

"Kaelin." Nick pulled her in for a hug and she went into his embrace with a rush of emotion at seeing him again. Despite the lingering embarrassment and betrayal at what she'd caught him doing, she couldn't hate Nick. He seemed happy to see her too, and she'd always felt he was a kindred spirit, still a friend even though she hadn't seen him for nearly ten years. Though she had to admit, his bulked-up body didn't inspire thoughts of friendship. She drew back. Nick too, had changed.

"Look at you," she said, brushing a hand over his close-cropped head. He was as close to being shaved bald as you could be, and it suited him. "What happened to your hair? And where'd you get all those muscles?"

He grinned. "Working out."

Her gaze tracked down over thickly muscled shoulders, rounded biceps and strong forearms, then over his broad, hard chest in a snug T-shirt. "Clearly." She smiled back at him. "You look great."

"Thanks. So you do."

She smiled and gave him a small eye roll.

"Seriously, Kaelin." Nick looked her up and down appreciatively, and her body tightened. "You were always pretty. Now you're just plain gorgeous."

She laughed at his outrageous compliment and shook her head.

"When did you get into town?" She changed the subject.

"Just a little while ago." Nick glanced at Tyler, who was watching them from beneath lowered brows, arms folded across his chest. "We drove down this afternoon."

Tyler and Nick lived in Chicago, a few hours away. You'd

think it was the other side of the world for how often they came home. But then Tyler never had been one to do what was expected of him. Such as visit his parents once in a while. She knew they'd had a rocky relationship, but everyone grew up sometime, surely, and his parents weren't getting any younger. Whatever. His life.

"I hear your business is doing well." She spoke to both men, her gaze moving back and forth between them. She didn't want to let on to Tyler how much she knew about his life now, but it was reasonable that she'd know at least that much from Avery.

Nick shot Tyler a narrow-eyed glance and a tight smile, but he nodded. "Yeah. So far, so good."

Oh-oh. She sensed something beneath the surface, but Tyler was already moving on, so clearly she wasn't going to find out what.

"And you're still living here in Mapleglen," Tyler said. She nodded. "I hear you're a lawyer."

"No." She pushed down the twinge of regret at his words. "Not a lawyer. Just a paralegal."

"Not *just* a paralegal," Nick said, bumping her with his shoulder. "I'm sure you're a great paralegal."

She smiled. "Yes. Yes I am." She turned back to Tyler. "I didn't go to law school, but I did get a job at a law firm here in town. Bickford Long." She knew he'd recognize the name since her boss, Paul Bickford, was a good friend of his dad. She held his gaze steadily, chin up, waiting for his mocking comment about where she worked, the small-town ultraconservative law firm. He'd always teased her about being a good girl—studious, serious, cautious. She fit right in at Bickford Long. Sort of.

"Yeah, I'd heard you work there. That's great," he said.

She blinked.

She liked her job, but it certainly wasn't exciting like his career. Apparently he was like a rock star in the advertising business in Chicago and had recently decided to open his own agency. Nick, an accountant, had joined as his partner. She knew the basics from one of Nick's emails but she hadn't wanted to ask too many questions about Tyler. But it had been easy to follow Tyler's career on Google, though shame burned through her at the fact that she'd done so, keeping track of him all these years. It wasn't surprising that he hadn't done the same to her, but the reality was, even if he *had* Googled her, there'd be nothing to find. Her life was pretty basic, living in the small city of Mapleglen, working at the law firm, visiting at the seniors' home with Taz, helping with church activities. Much of her adult life had been spent caring for her parents, but they were gone now.

"Okay, you can all catch up later!" Avery interrupted them, taking Kaelin's arm and squeezing it in a hug. "Kaelin needs to come upstairs and see my dress." She dragged Kaelin away from the others, out into the hall and then up the stairs. "Thank you so much for everything you've done," she chatted, leading the way. "I could never have organized this wedding without you."

"I think your mom could've handled it," Kaelin replied dryly. She'd had some challenges with Mrs. Wirth throughout this whole deal.

"But she wouldn't have done what I wanted!"

"True that," Kaelin said with heartfelt agreement. The wedding would have been completely different if Mrs. Wirth had her way. Kaelin didn't think she'd ever met anyone so concerned with what people thought, with making a good impression, putting on a show. Well, besides Dr. Wirth, just as preoccupied with image as his wife. Kaelin had had to use every ounce of her negotiation and persuasion skills to keep Mrs.

Wirth from turning the wedding into an over-the-top, blow-the-bank spectacle.

"She only has one daughter," Avery continued, walking into the room that had been her bedroom, where the two of them had spent so many teenage hours. "That's what she keeps telling me. And it doesn't look like Tyler will be getting married any time soon."

Kaelin sank her teeth into her bottom lip and strove for casual. "No? No girlfriend?"

Avery shrugged. "He was going out with someone last time I visited him in Chicago, but he didn't want to bring anyone to the wedding, so I guess not."

Kaelin couldn't even identify all the feelings swirling inside her at that comment.

Avery walked into the closet and returned with her dress. "Here it is!"

Kaelin gazed at the dress, then back at Avery. "This is it?"

Avery frowned. "Yes. I know it doesn't look like much on the hanger, but when I put it on you'll see. And it looks pretty plain, but I have these necklaces that go with it..." She laid the dress on the bed and rushed over to the dresser. Kaelin stroked a hand over the strapless column of ivory taffeta. The dress was very simple—no ruffles, lace or tulle, not a pouf or sparkle in sight.

"It's beautiful, Avery. What did your mom think of it?"

"She hasn't seen it." Avery turned around, several long strands of pearls and rhinestones dangling from her hands. "I told her she has to wait until the wedding day."

Kaelin laughed. "Isn't that the groom who has to wait until the wedding day to see you?"

Avery grinned. "You know I'm not superstitious."

"You mean he's seen the dress?" Kaelin's mouth dropped open.

Avery laughed. "No! I'm not superstitious, but I still want him to be blown away when he sees me on Saturday."

Kaelin laughed too. "Okay," she said. "I think I can visualize it. Very nice."

"My mom's going to be disappointed," Avery said, turning back to tuck the jewelry away. "But it's my wedding."

And that's why Kaelin had had to fight...er...negotiate with Mrs. Wirth over so many things. She almost felt sorry for Mrs. Wirth, her disappointment so huge at not being able to put on the ostentatious show she wanted to, but Kaelin's loyalty was with her best friend. She'd spent exhausting hours, though, placating Mrs. Wirth, trying to make her feel better.

"Since you came all the way back here to Illinois to get married in your family church, I expected a more traditional dress," Kaelin commented. "But it's beautiful, it really is."

Avery made a face, her pretty mouth twisting. "I'm probably crazy to be doing this, with my family. We should have eloped."

Kaelin met her eyes. She knew things had been tense in the Wirth family for many years. Tyler had spent most of his teenage years provoking his parents, wild rumors flying about him that could have been true or could have been him trying to piss his parents off. And now he never came home. She'd always wondered if it had anything to do with what she'd walked in on that night, but how could it? She was the only one who'd seen them and she'd certainly never told a soul. The stabbing pain she'd first felt at seeing Tyler and Nick with another girl like that had faded to a dull ache.

"Oh, Ave, honey," she said, moving toward her friend. "This is what you wanted, isn't it?"

"Well, it's too late to change things."

18

That wasn't an answer. Dammit. Kaelin's heart sank. "What do you want to change?"

"Oh, Kaelin." Avery sighed. "I don't want to change my wedding. I just want to change my family. Things are so tense." She swallowed. "I hoped...I wanted...aw shit."

Kaelin gazed searchingly at her friend, holding both her hands. Secrets between them remained unspoken but almost physically tangible, things Kaelin hadn't shared with her best friend from that summer ten years ago, things she'd always had a feeling Avery was keeping from her too. She searched for the right thing to say, the right question to ask.

"Tense?" she finally said, her voice tight. "Why?"

Avery pulled back and her eyes dropped. She picked up her wedding dress. "Oh you know, just the usual. Mom's disappointed in the wedding, but she's still trying so hard to impress Scott's parents. And now Tyler's here, you know how he likes to push their buttons. But at least it will take the heat off me."

Kaelin choked on a laugh. "And isn't that always the way it was?" Avery, a perfect angel in her parents' eyes, could do no wrong compared to Tyler's tumultuous teenage antics.

"Hell yeah. And they're so annoyed that Nick is here too."

Kaelin went still and tense. "Why would they be annoyed about that?"

"Oh. Who knows?" Avery waved a hand and quickly changed the subject. "I'll show you my shoes."

Kaelin hated this, hated these unspoken things between them, things that had hung between them for ten years. She suspected Avery knew something about what had happened, but wouldn't talk about it for reasons of her own, and Kaelin wasn't about to tell her in case she didn't know. Because it was Tyler and Nick's secret too. Well, and the girl they'd been with.

19

That old ache intensified. It had also been humiliating, how devastated she'd been, something too painful to talk about for years, and after a few years, it was just weird to bring it up. So the secrets stayed hidden away.

She pushed those thoughts away, a wave of heat sweeping over her.

As Avery turned back toward her, she gave her friend a bright smile. "Oh yes, please, I want to see your shoes. And what about your veil?"

Tyler watched his sister lead Kaelin out of the room.

Kaelin.

He sucked in air and picked up the drink he'd set down on the coffee table, took a gulp of burning Scotch.

He fucking hated Scotch.

He should have picked up beer on the way over from the hotel. He should have known his dad wouldn't have beer for the party. Beer was too low-class for him.

"Let's all go out on the deck!" his mother urged everyone, flitting around the room. "It's such a lovely evening, we'll have our drinks and hors d'oeuvres out by the pool."

More guests were supposed to arrive, friends and family arriving in town for the wedding. Mom was dressed in a silk dress and high heels, and Tyler could feel the desperation of her need to impress her future in-laws. Christ, how embarrassing.

On top of that, there was the sharp edge of displeasure Tyler felt from his parents now that he was there, that chilly stiffness, the awkwardness at finally coming home after all those years, after the gut-wrenching way he'd left. That old bitterness and resentment inside him that had never fully faded away ate away at his insides.

How the hell was he going to survive the next few days?

With lots of Scotch. He tossed back the rest of his drink then felt Nick's eyes on him.

"You okay?" Nick asked in a low voice.

Tyler grimaced. "Yeah."

Scott and his parents went outside with the other guests, leaving them alone.

"I know you didn't want to come home."

"I can handle it. And what am I supposed to do, miss my sister's wedding?"

"I didn't have to come."

Tyler shook his head slowly from side to side. "You were invited. Avery invited you. Of course you had to come."

"I mean, I didn't have to come here, to the house. Today."

"Oh."

Nick swirled the remains of his own drink in the glass. "It pisses your parents off."

Tyler grinned. "I know. Bonus!"

Nick laughed.

"I should go tell the girls everyone's outside," Tyler said.

Nick snorted. "Bullshit. Like they won't find us when they come down." He caught Tyler's eye. "You're still hung up on her, aren't you?"

Chapter Two

"What? Who?" But he knew there was no fooling Nick. The guy knew him, inside and out.

"You know who. She looks good."

Tyler's chest tightened. Of course she looked good. She'd always looked good.

Other than that day...fuck. His stomach still swooped every time he remembered Kaelin walking in on him and Nick and Tracy Brown. He'd known it was risky, doing what they were doing right there in the family room. His parents and Avery had been out, not expected home for hours, but still, the possibility that they could walk in on them had added an edge of danger to the whole scene, increased the thrill factor. And Kaelin showing up hadn't actually been a complete surprise.

But when Tyler had looked up and seen her standing there open-mouthed, frozen, he'd been shocked at how truly god-awful he'd felt, seeing the hurt on her face, his guts twisting into knots, his heart squeezing painfully.

"She still thinks we're depraved assholes," he muttered.

Nick rubbed his forehead. "We are."

Tyler snorted. "Yeah. True enough." Then he sighed.

"Actually," Nick said, "I didn't get that vibe from her."

"Of course you don't. It's just me. She always hated me.

That just sealed the deal." Nick opened his mouth to speak, but Tyler rushed on. "And what was with the big bear hug?" he demanded before Nick could say something stupid, like some kind of stupid denial that Kaelin had hated him. Because he didn't want to hear that, or think about that, or feel that goddamn guilt again. "Like you're long lost friends."

"We *are* friends," Nick said quietly. "I always liked Kaelin."

"Yeah." Bitterness edged Tyler's voice. "I know."

Nick laughed. "You're fucking jealous, man! I can't believe it."

"I am not." He scowled.

"Yeah, you are. For Chrissakes, Ty, I can't believe you still have a thing for her after all these years."

"A thing?" Tyler laughed. "What the hell does that mean? I don't have 'a thing' for her."

"Whatever. Come on, we better join the others."

They went outside. Tyler accepted another drink, only because it was alcohol and he needed it to get through this ordeal. His irritation increased as he found himself continually looking at the doors to the patio, waiting for Avery and Kaelin to rejoin them. He half listened to his mother telling Scott's parents about the new furniture she'd just bought for the patio, how they'd had to put in a special rush order so they'd have it for the wedding.

God, he just wanted to get this wedding over with and get the hell back to Chicago. Although, there were nothing but problems waiting for him there too. He and Nick were in the middle of a massive difference of opinion on a potential client who wanted to sign with them. A *big* potential client, *huge* potential client with lots of money to spend on advertising that could really get their fledgling agency off the ground. Shit.

But he was here for Avery, his big sister, happy for her that she'd found a great guy like Scott. Though he wished with all his heart she and Scott had just eloped. What the hell was she thinking, planning a big family wedding that was torture for everyone? Tyler took a big swallow of Scotch as Avery appeared in the French doors, followed by Kaelin.

His eyes went straight to her. So pretty. So different from Avery. Not the pretty part—his sister was pretty too, he supposed, but in a different way. Avery was all blonde highlights and makeup; Kaelin was a sweep of silky brown hair and big brown eyes. In high school she'd been an intimidating overachiever, top marks, all kinds of academic awards, involved in the student council and about a dozen different clubs and committees. Just like Avery.

Tyler'd been disturbed to find that, as he entered his teenage years and started thinking about girls differently, he'd started thinking about his big sister's best friend differently. She'd always been at their place, as comfortable as if she lived there. Memory of one morning when he'd encountered her in the upstairs hallway after she'd slept over with Avery had fueled his hormone-driven fantasies for years. She'd been wearing tiny little plaid shorts that revealed her long, smooth legs, which okay, he'd seen many times in the summer, but also a ribbed cotton tank top *with no bra.* She had great tits, high and full and round with prominent nipples, and the sight had sent him back to his room for a fast and furious hand job.

From his seat in a corner of the patio, he watched her now, smiling and laughing and making conversation with the other guests. Her blue and beige plaid sundress was far from revealing, with its full knee-length skirt and modest straps. But it did show off a lot of smooth bare skin—arms, shoulders, a faint hint of cleavage, the snug bodice hugging her breasts and small waist. She accepted a glass of wine from his dad, earning

24

a smile of approval from him that Tyler'd never seen directed his way. He frowned. Everyone loved Kaelin. So polite, so responsible.

"Would you snap out of it!"

Tyler jerked at Nick's low-voiced command, and looked up at his friend standing there. He frowned. "What?"

"Everyone's afraid to talk to you. You look like you're going to snap their head off if they say a word to you, sitting there scowling like that. Would you at least try to act normal?"

Only Nick would say that to him. Only Nick could get away with talking to him like that. Anyone else, he'd be pounding the shit out of him. With a sigh, he rose and moved toward the others, a smile firmly in place, and made conversation with the soon-to-be in-laws.

More guests arrived, which in a way was good, because it kept his parents too busy playing host and hostess to bug him. His mom was pulling out all the stops. She must have been cooking for days, which he knew she loved, but still, it was a lot. Also a full bar setup outside, torches and lights and candles around the glowing turquoise pool in their backyard.

When he found himself face-to-face with Kaelin, somehow, their glances collided and bounced away from each other. Tyler's skin tingled. He licked his lips and searched for something to say.

Kaelin looked down at the glass of wine in her hand. After the conversation she and Avery had just had about Tyler, now he was right there in front of her. She had to put all that old crap out of her head and act like an adult.

"Avery says you've been busy helping with this wedding," Tyler said, still all chilly politeness, as if *she* was the one who'd done something wrong.

25

"I was happy to help. With her living in Los Angeles, it would have been impossible to get things done."

He nodded. "That was nice of you."

Oh yeah, here it came, the sardonic comments about how nice she was, what a good girl she was. She waited, her gaze flickering up to his. But he didn't say it. "Um. Thanks."

"When's the rest of the wedding party getting here? I thought there were three bridesmaids."

Men. He didn't even know who else was in the wedding party. "Just two. Me, and Avery's friend in L.A., Maddie. Scott's best man, Hardeep, is her boyfriend. They should be here tonight."

"Just two, huh?" He nodded, looked out over the pool.

"Your mom wanted her to have ten."

His head snapped around, eyes wide. "Ten?"

She smiled. "Yep."

He rolled his eyes. "Jesus Christ."

Their gazes held for a moment of shared amusement and understanding. Kaelin felt a wave of heat wash over her body and her skin tightened and tingled. Tension hummed between them, memories of that summer flooding back.

"Well, my goodness, Tyler! I haven't seen you in forever!" An older woman approached them and gave Tyler a hug.

"Hi, Aunt Mona." Tyler smiled. "It has been a while, hasn't it? But I think you look even younger. How is that possible?"

Mona giggled. Giggled! A fifty-year-old woman with dyed red hair and a double-D bosom giggled like a pre-teen girl. "Oh, you," she said, fluttering her eyelashes. "I hear you're doing well in Chicago. Your mom tells us about all the big, important clients you have and how much money you're making."

"She does?" Tyler's eyebrows drew together.

26

"She talks about you all the time! So proud of you."

Now his eyebrows flew up and he made a choking sound. "I'll bet," he muttered just as Mona turned to Kaelin.

"Kaelin. How are you, dear?"

"I'm fine, thanks." She smiled at the other lady.

"Where's your young man tonight?"

"There is no young man, Mona. We sort of...broke up."

"But I just saw you together the other day!"

"Yes, well." Kaelin glanced uncomfortably at Tyler taking in their conversation with a frown. "We're still friends."

"I thought you were getting married."

Kaelin shifted position, acutely aware of Tyler's interest. "We were," she mumbled. "But it wasn't going to work out." She straightened her shoulders and gave Mona a bright smile. "We're both fine with it."

Mona shook her head sadly. "That boy is crazy about you, Kaelin. And he's a good catch! A police officer. Good steady job, a nice boy."

Kaelin caught Tyler's eye roll and her stomach tightened.

"You know, I'm so glad to see you," Mona continued, blithely unaware of the tension snapping between Kaelin and Tyler. "I need one more person to work an hour at the church bake sale next weekend."

Kaelin wanted to close her eyes. The church bake sale. Could Mona make her life sound any more pathetic to Tyler? "Next weekend," she repeated. "Not this coming weekend."

"Oh no, of course not! This weekend is the wedding! This is the wedding of the year in Mapleglen! It's next Saturday. We need someone there for nine in the morning."

Kaelin smiled tightly. "Sure. I can help."

"Thank you, dear. You're such a good girl." Mona patted her cheek. "Now I must go meet that handsome groom of Avery's."

Kaelin tossed down the last of her wine in three big gulps, again waiting for Tyler's amusement. This time he didn't disappoint.

"A police officer, huh?"

She met his gaze head-on. "Yes."

"A nice boy," he repeated.

Kaelin pressed her lips together.

"How come you broke up?"

She did not want to talk about this to Tyler. In fact, she almost wished she'd let Brent talk her into bringing him along tonight. A boyfriend beside her would have gone a long way to helping her deal with Tyler.

But she didn't really have a boyfriend and she wasn't going to tell Tyler why exactly things hadn't worked out between them. Brent kept calling her, dropping in to see her, still hopeful that she was going to change her mind, but deep down inside she knew that wasn't going to happen.

"That's not really your business," she said stiffly.

"Sounds like he'd be perfect for you," Tyler continued. "Since you're such a good girl."

His words ricocheted around in her head, memories of teenage Tyler mocking her about how good she was, laughing at her for being disappointed because she'd gotten a B+ on a test, making fun of her for spending Saturday night studying. She remembered how Tyler's teasing had started to bug her because...well, because it was *him*. Because she didn't always *want* to spend Saturday nights studying, but she didn't have a crazy social life like he did, and because sometimes she had no choice, she *had* to stay home on Saturday nights. Remembered hurt and frustration rushed through her.

She fought for control of her surging emotions and lifted her wineglass again. Empty. Dammit.

"You probably don't want another glass of wine," Tyler said. "One's your limit, right?"

She lifted her eyes to his face. "You're still an asshole," she said quietly.

His jaw tightened, though he kept his smile in place. "Yep," he said. "I sure am. Are you surprised about that?"

"No," she said. She tipped her head. "Though I don't know why you feel a need to take out your frustrations on me. I never did anything to you."

His smile disappeared. "Frustrations?"

Now he looked pissed.

Good.

"Yes. You obviously have some deep-seated sense of inferiority that makes you need to make fun of others to make yourself feel better."

His mouth dropped open. "What the fuck." His eyes narrowed, flashing blue sparks at her.

"Oh, don't even look at me like that," she said. "You have no right to be mad at me. I'm the one who should be mad."

"Oh for Chrissake. Lighten up a little. You always were Miss Serious."

They faced each other, glaring. Kaelin's fingers curled tightly around the stem of her wineglass, almost snapping it. He thought she was upset about him teasing her! Jesus, how stupid could one man be? Did he not even realize what he'd done?

But there'd never been anything real between them. As

they'd spent time together that summer, her feelings for Tyler had grown into something they shouldn't have, and when he'd kissed her—just once—she'd foolishly believed he was starting to feel the same about her.

And the very next day she'd walked in on that scene.

She fought to control the long-suppressed rage surging inside her, shocked by a desire to hurt him back. The urge to physically hit him, the way she'd wanted to that night. Before she'd run out of the house then run all the way out of Mapleglen and back to college, a week early. And then to her horror, her hand lifted, swung back—and she did it.

Right in the middle of a big party of friends and family, she slapped Tyler Wirth's face.

Chapter Three

Tyler automatically lifted a hand to his smarting cheek and rubbed it, stunned into speechlessness. Kaelin stood there, big brown eyes wide, mouth in an O of horror. The chatter of the guests faded into silence, only the faint saxophone strains of the jazz CD playing quietly on the outdoor speakers drifting on the evening air.

Jesus fucking Christ. She did *not* just do that.

The two of them stared at each other, the air around them hot enough to burst into flames.

"Omigod," she said. She closed her eyes. Opened them. "Omigod."

She turned as if she was going to run, and he reached out and grabbed her upper arm. "Oh no, you don't," he said through gritted teeth, heat still stinging his face.

"Tyler." His mother appeared at his side and he became aware of everyone around them, gawking at them as if they were a car wreck on the freeway. Shit. He glanced at his mom, took in the tightening of her mouth, the snapping in her eyes. "What are you doing?" She hissed the words out quietly.

What was *he* doing? What the fuck? He was the one who just got decked!

Nick appeared now, too, calm, controlled. He looked back

and forth between him and Kaelin.

"I am so sorry," Kaelin whispered to Tyler's mom. "I didn't intend to cause a scene."

Mom looked at Kaelin. "What did he say to you?"

Kaelin just stared back at her and shook her head. "I—it wasn't his fault," she finally stammered, shocking Tyler. His mom cast a look of disbelief his way. Of course it was his fault. It was always his fault.

"I'm outta here," he muttered, trying to push his way past Nick. "Let's go."

But Nick didn't move, despite Tyler's shove, and then Avery arrived, her eyes wide and darting back and forth between everyone.

"Don't go, Tyler," she begged. "Please." She grabbed hold of his arm. "Come with me."

He let his sister drag him to the far end of the deck. Chatter started humming again as people began talking, punctuated with a couple of nervous titters. He couldn't help but follow Kaelin with his eyes even as Avery talked to him.

"Please, Tyler, don't go," she said. "It's my wedding and I want you here."

He watched his mom pat Kaelin's shoulder reassuringly before going back to her other guests. He watched Nick standing there, head bent to Kaelin, talking to her.

What the fuck was he saying?

"Tyler." Avery pushed at his shoulder.

He tried to focus on her. "Why do you want me here?" he demanded. "It's just making everyone nuts."

"You're my brother," she said, voice thick and teary. "And I'm getting married. And I want my family with me. *All* of my family."

Christ, what was he supposed to say to that? She was his sister and it wasn't her fault he was such an asshole that he got slapped in the middle of a party. He rubbed his face, hardly able to believe sweet little Kaelin Daume had done that.

And created quite a scene. A girl who lived her life as carefully as possible so as not to attract attention or risk embarrassment. Wow. He looked over at her again, nodding to Nick.

A slow smile tugged his mouth.

"Why did Kaelin slap you?"

He focused back on Avery. "Because I was being an asshole to her. As usual."

She frowned. "God, Tyler, haven't you grown up yet? You always did like to yank her chain. Geez, you were like a little boy with a crush…" Her voice trailed off and her gaze sharpened. Tyler's gut tightened. He looked away from her penetrating gaze. Avery opened her mouth to speak, and he shot her a glare. She closed her mouth.

"Well," she said. "Then I guess you deserved it."

"Of course I did. I always do. Right?"

She sighed and closed her eyes briefly. "I'm not so sure of that. Why do you just keep digging yourself deeper?"

"I have no fucking idea what you're talking about." He smiled. "I'll stay, but just for you, Sis. Just keep me away from Mom and Dad or I might kill them."

"And away from Kaelin, apparently," she murmured.

He couldn't stand it. What were Kaelin and Nick talking about over there? Without him? Probably about him and what a jerk he was. "I'll behave," he promised Avery, moving back toward Kaelin and Nick as if drawn by a powerful magnet.

He stopped beside them and they both looked at him.

His gaze glanced off Nick and landed on Kaelin. Fuck, why did he keep hurting her? What was wrong with him?

"I'm sorry," she said. "I shouldn't have done that."

"No, I'm sorry. I was being a jerk."

Kaelin and Nick exchanged glances that confirmed his suspicions about what they'd been discussing.

"I'm kinda tense right now." Tyler rubbed the back of his neck, keeping his voice low. "It isn't easy coming back here after all this time."

"Well, maybe you should come home a little more often," Kaelin snapped. "I'm sure your parents miss you."

Fuck. She had no idea what had happened. And he wasn't about to tell her. "I doubt it," he snarled.

"If I leave you two to go get us drinks, will another brawl break out?" Nick interjected.

Kaelin wrinkled her nose at him adorably. Sure, for *Nick.* "Of course not."

Nick nodded and headed to the bar. Kaelin twisted her fingers together. Sticky silence surrounded them, there in the middle of a noisy party.

"That was about more than just my bugging you, wasn't it?" He met her eyes.

She held his gaze but didn't answer, and her pretty bottom lip quivered. And made him want to kiss it. "Fuck," he muttered, dropping his head. His neck and shoulders were as hard as stone, that tight pain spreading up the back of his scalp. What could he say to her? How could he ever explain things?"

"It was a long time ago," she said, her words clipped short. "It doesn't matter."

He lifted his head to look at her again. "Ah, Kaelin. You

have changed."

She lowered her chin. "You think?"

He smiled. "The Kaelin Daume I knew would never have slapped a guy's face. Especially in the middle of a party."

She licked her lips and it was so fucking sexy he forgot to breathe. "Well," she said. "I don't think that's a good thing. And you've changed too."

He lifted an eyebrow. "I thought we just established that I'm still an asshole." Her cheeks went pink and he shrugged. "I've been called worse."

She bit her lip and looked up at him through her eyelashes. "I mean you've changed because you actually apologized. And admitted you were acting like a jerk."

His mouth twisted and he had to fight the urge to shut her up by slamming his mouth over hers.

Nick returned carrying three glasses, handed one to Tyler and a wineglass to Kaelin. "Here," he said. "I think we can all use this."

"What is it? More Scotch?" Tyler grimaced.

Nick grinned. "Sorry, bud."

"Better make sure there's gonna be beer at the wedding," Tyler said and took a swallow. His eyes damn near watered. "Avery!" he called to his sister. She turned, gave him a look, held up a finger as she finished a conversation with Aunt Mona.

"There will be beer," Kaelin said. "I should know, since I booked everything."

Tyler slid his arm around her shoulders and pulled her in for a hug. "Oh, thank Christ."

He hadn't thought before he'd done it, just reacted, but the feel of her soft, warm body against his, the smell of her hair, a sweet, fruity, floral scent that filled his senses, almost took him out at the knees and stalled his breath. He wanted to press his mouth to the top of her silky head, wrap her up and... His eyes met Nick's over Kaelin's head, Nick's steady, knowing gaze, and he released Kaelin and stepped back.

She blinked and tugged at the neckline of her dress, cheeks even pinker now.

Avery arrived and her gaze tracked over Kaelin's flushed cheeks, and Tyler's own face heated up. "What's up?"

"I was going to ask if there'd be beer at the reception, but Kaelin tells me there will be."

Avery laughed. "Beer. Gawd, Tyler. Come on, my other bridesmaid just arrived. Come and meet her."

Nick and Kaelin followed brother and sister to the French doors into the house where Scott's best man Hardeep and his girlfriend Maddie stood. Kaelin had met Avery's new friend a few times. She liked her, but sometimes it was hard not to feel left out when she and Avery talked about all the things they now had in common that Kaelin wasn't part of. Plus, with Maddie and Hardeep being a couple, and Hardeep and Scott being good friends, the four of them spent a lot of time together. Maddie lived in Avery's new world, with other friends Kaelin didn't know. Although Kaelin and Avery shared a history and they would always be friends, their relationship had changed.

Last time Kaelin had visited Avery in Los Angeles, Avery had suggested Kaelin move there. "Don't be silly," Kaelin had said. "I can't move away from Mapleglen."

"Why not? Seriously. Your mom and dad are gone now. You can easily get a job here at some law firm."

Kaelin looked down at her wineglass now, remembering how ridiculous and scary that thought had been, and yet...her life in Mapleglen was not the life she somehow had anticipated living. She didn't even know exactly what she wanted, but she knew there was a hole in her life, an empty dissatisfaction that shifted from mild discontent to aching loneliness.

Maybe she should think about that idea again.

"Okay?" Nick asked in a low voice for her alone.

She smiled at him. "Of course."

He'd talked to her after she'd slapped Tyler, made sure she was okay, agreed with her that Tyler could be a real jerk, made her laugh. And then he'd hugged her and a warm rush of affection had flowed through her. Well, and a little tingle of something else. Nick was really buff, big and strong and hard.

And so was Tyler. She sighed, thinking about her body's reaction to Tyler's casual hug. Man, maybe she should go back to Brent, just so they could sleep together. She was obviously sex-deprived. But sadly, sex with Brent hadn't been all that great.

Avery introduced people and fetched drinks, and the evening sped by in a blur of conversation and laughter, a lingering awareness sparking her nerves every time she and Tyler locked glances, or she and Nick shared a smile.

"We're heading out now," Nick murmured to her later. "Guess we'll see you tomorrow."

"Oh. You're not staying here at the house?"

Nick shook his head. "No. Tyler wanted to stay at the hotel."

"At the Red Maple Inn?"

"Yeah."

"Oh. Well. That's good, you'll be right there for the wedding. And the rehearsal dinner tomorrow night. Mrs. Wirth has booked a private room there for dinner."

"I won't be at the rehearsal dinner."

"Oh." The dinner was the one part of the weekend Kaelin hadn't had a hand in planning. Avery had allowed her mom to do whatever she wanted for the rehearsal dinner. Kaelin licked her lips, and looked up at Nick. "I guess it's just for the wedding party."

"Yeah." He smiled. "No big deal. I can amuse myself for an evening."

"I'm sure you still have some friends here." Nick's parents had moved away a few years ago, she knew, which was why he had an excuse for never coming back even if Tyler didn't.

"Yeah. A few."

Tyler walked up. "Ready to go?"

"Yup." Guests had started leaving a while ago and the party was winding down.

"I told Avery I'll help with whatever she needs done tomorrow," Tyler said. "Apparently there's all kind of shit to do—picking up decorations and crap."

Kaelin grinned. "Yeah. Avery will be busy having her spa day."

Tyler rolled his eyes. "I suppose you're going with her."

"Yes." She sighed. "It's not my thing, but Avery insisted on treating Maddie and me to manicures and pedicures and some kind of body scrub thing."

Tyler eyed her body and heat followed his gaze.

"If you're picking up the decorations, you can bring them to my place," she said. "So I can take them on Saturday."

"Where do you live, Kaelin?" Nick asked.

"Same place. My parents' house."

"Okay."

"So I guess I'll see you tomorrow," she rushed on a bit

breathlessly.

She watched the two men leave out the front door, her nerves twitching, skin tingling. Exhaustion fell over her like a heavy blanket. Wow, what a roller coaster ride of an evening. Seeing Tyler again had her emotions all over the place, leaving her both drained and excited.

Bad. It was so bad.

She'd been so focused on pulling off this wedding for her best friend, making it everything Avery wanted it to be, she'd barely even thought about what it was going to be like to see Tyler and Nick again. It added a whole other dimension to everything, an unexpected, unsettling dimension. She covered her face with one hand briefly and lowered it just as Avery approached her. Avery wrapped her arms around her and hugged her.

"I'm sorry about the scene, Ave," Kaelin said, hugging her best friend back.

"Don't even worry about it. Every party needs a little excitement."

"I don't think your mom would agree."

Avery snorted. "You know what she's like." She released Kaelin. "What was that about anyway?"

"Um...you mean with Tyler?"

"Yeah." Avery's searching gaze had Kaelin turning away to pick up some empty glasses off a table.

"Oh, he just drives me crazy." She tried for a light and casual laugh but nearly choked on it. Avery followed her into the kitchen with more dishes.

"Mmmm." Her noncommittal response made Kaelin nervous. "He's such an intense guy."

"Intense?" Kaelin shot Avery a glance over her shoulder

from the dishwasher. "That's not a word I would have used to describe Tyler. He always seems like he doesn't give a shit about anything."

"He *seems* that way," she agreed. "So. Let's talk about what's happening tomorrow."

The party finally over, the guests all gone, the kitchen spotless once again, Margot poured herself one last glass of wine. Ken had already gone up to bed, but she needed a few minutes to wind down. Her nerves were stretched taut, her face hurt from the smile she'd kept firmly in place all evening and she was exhausted from making small talk and her constant efforts to make sure every detail of the party was perfect. She really had to get over that, but it wasn't so easy to let go of the few things she felt control over in her life.

She also wanted to sit down and think about her son.

Tyler. He'd walked into the house and her heart had leaped with joy at the sight of him. He was a man now, taller than his father, broader than his father, though with the same lean athletic build. Everyone said both her children looked like her, with blond hair and blue eyes, but she saw Ken's strong jaw and high cheekbones in Tyler's handsome face. She longed to run her hand over his cheek, as she had when he was small, to enfold him in a hug, except now he was a good seven inches taller and probably sixty pounds heavier than she. She smiled wistfully and carried her glass of wine toward her office.

But Tyler hadn't been so happy to see her. Her heart constricted remembering his cool greeting, the way he'd rebuffed her attempt to hug him, the way he'd avoided her and any attempts to talk to him all evening. Now she ached, deep down inside, a sad painful ache.

She shouldn't check her email again. There'd been nothing from him earlier, and now it was after midnight there likely wasn't now. But she knew she was going to. Because chatting with him, telling him about her children, telling him what had happened with Tyler without having to hold anything back, was a bright glowing spot in her bleak, exhausting evening.

She opened the door to her office and stopped short in the doorway. Her husband sat at her computer. He turned to her, his eyebrows drawn into a bewildered frown, his mouth open. "Margot."

Her heart actually stopped, and she put a hand to her chest as it then hurdled into a rapid, uneven rhythm. "What are you doing?" She thought he'd gone to bed.

"What are *you* doing?" he asked slowly, gesturing to her computer. "Who is this man you've been emailing with?"

Her mouth went dry and she swallowed. "Just a friend."

He rose to his feet and stood here, looking back and forth between her and the computer. "You never mentioned a friend."

"Ken." How could she explain this to him? Why did she feel guilty? She'd never met Jeff in person. It was just a friendship, as she'd said. Someone to talk to and laugh with and maybe even flirt a little, but it had never gone beyond that.

He gazed at her and moved his head slowly from side to side. "Margot. I don't understand what's been happening with you."

"I've tried to tell you," she whispered. She clutched the glass of wine in both trembling hands. "I've tried."

He squinted at her, as if having trouble seeing her. Since their children had both left home, she'd been increasingly unhappy with her life. She'd tried to keep busy, with the charity work she knew Ken liked her to do, with her golf and tennis and her friends. Shopping and decorating the house. But lately it

41

hadn't been enough.

The most embarrassing thing was that she wanted sex. Lots of sex. All the time. She'd chalked it up to some premenopausal hormonal surge. She'd bought sexy lingerie and tried to seduce her husband. It worked. Just not as much as she wanted it to. Perhaps sex every day was a little unrealistic for a sixty-year-old man, but she still believed a couple of times a week was reasonable. Wasn't it?

Now they had no children around, no reason not to have sex anytime, anywhere they wanted it, but Ken still worked long hours, still came home tired. The frustration from that built on her long-buried hopes and dreams for her life.

"You said you wanted me to retire," he said now.

"And you said you don't want to." She'd suggested they could travel. Maybe to Europe. Australia. Thailand. She'd always wanted to go to Thailand. He'd thought she was nuts.

"I'm not ready to retire. And I don't understand this..." He threw out a hand toward her computer. "Why?"

She moved across the room on stiff legs. As if it hadn't been stressful enough with Tyler coming home, disappointing her with his cool demeanor, and then he and Kaelin having that awful blowup, now she had to deal with this.

"I was going to talk to you after the wedding," she said, sitting on the small couch. She looked down at her wine. "I don't think I can go on like this."

He stared at her, hands hanging at his sides. "What are you saying, Margot?"

"I'm saying...I don't know." She closed her eyes. Did she have the nerve to leave him? Probably not. Where would she go? What would she do? "I just wanted to get the wedding over with and then talk about it. I'm not happy, Ken."

His face actually paled. He blinked at her. She'd kind of thought that if she left, he might not even notice.

But yes, he would, because he needed a wife to be out in the community, all smiling and happy and doing charity work and putting on a show of living the life he thought they should live.

"I haven't been happy for a long time. You knew that." She kept her voice soft.

She'd tried to explain to him how she felt, but he hadn't wanted to hear it. He'd never been one to talk about feelings, always wanted to ignore problems. Which was probably why talking online to someone like Jeff had been so easy, so appealing. So dangerous.

Ken still just stood there. He turned back to the computer, where she'd apparently forgotten to delete those last emails. And had left her email program open.

She sighed. They said when people made stupid mistakes like that it was because they wanted to get caught. Not that she'd cheated on him or anything. But maybe it was her subconscious trying to make her deal with this, after so many years of trying to push it so far below the surface.

"I haven't cheated on you," she said, voicing that thought. "He is just a friend. Someone to talk to." She pressed a hand to her aching forehead. "I can't do this right now. But after the wedding...Ken, we seriously have to talk."

He left the room, and she heard him climbing the stairs with slow, measured steps, up to their room, upstairs where Avery was now sleeping in her girlhood bedroom. She leaned back and closed her eyes.

At the Red Maple Inn, Tyler and Nick walked into their room, flicking on lights.

"Fuck," Tyler said. "What a night." He let out a heartfelt sigh and fell onto the bed. He stared up at the ceiling. He'd been back in town, back with his family, less than a day, and already he'd started acting out all the tension and anger that simmered below the surface with his family. Shit.

"Want one of these?" Nick opened the small bar fridge and held up a beer.

"Nah. Had enough booze." He heard the fridge door close and then the bed dipped under Nick's weight as he sat beside him.

Silence settled around them. Tyler lifted his head and rubbed the back of his neck.

"Neck sore?" Nick asked.

"Hell yeah."

"Roll over."

Tyler turned away from Nick, face-down on the bed. Then Nick's hands found his shoulders and started massaging the tight muscles. His strong fingers dug into rock-like muscles and Tyler groaned.

"You always store all your tension here."

Tyler grunted a wordless response, his eyes closing. Then the bed shifted again and he felt Nick moving over him, straddling his ass, still kneading tight muscles, using his thumbs to work his way down his spine.

Tension seeped out of him. Some tension. But then a different kind of tension filled him at the feel of Nick's hands on his body and his muscled thighs against his hips. Tyler's dick swelled against the bed and he imagined Nick's doing the same, thickening and lengthening in his pants where he now pressed against his ass. He let the moan pass through his lips.

"Feel good?" Nick's hands kept moving on him—mesmerizing, sensual, arousing.

"Yeah."

Nick moved away. "Take your clothes off."

They both tossed off their clothes, and Tyler resumed his prone position, arms bent, and Nick straddled him again, this time bare skin to hot bare skin. Nick's cock rubbed up and down the crease of Tyler's ass as his hands moved up and down his back, over his tight shoulders. Every nerve ending in Tyler's ass jumped at the feel of Nick's cock sliding there, and his own dick hardened even more against the mattress.

Tyler jerked when Nick's tongue licked up his back, when his teeth nipped a shoulder muscle. He lifted his head as fire streaked through him, and Nick's hand slid over his forehead, pulling his head back even farther, and rubbed over his hair. Tyler groaned.

Nick bent low again, slid his hands beneath Tyler's arms and gripped his fists, cock sliding up and down, sending a barrage of sparks over those sensitive nerves, his body rubbing over Tyler's back, his face rubbing Tyler's face. If Nick's goal was to ease the tension in him, he'd succeeded, but fuck, he'd created a whole other kind of tension. Tyler's balls tightened and pressure built.

Still stretched over Tyler's back, Nick released Tyler's hands and slid his hands into Tyler's hair. He rubbed his nose against Tyler's cheek, paused, then licked around his ear. Sensation poured through Tyler, thick and hot. Nick pressed his face to Tyler's and they lay like that for a moment, the heat of Nick's cheek seeping into his face, the roughness of Nick's stubble scraping against his, the weight of Nick's body pressing him into the mattress, the sound of Nick's harsh breathing loud in his ear.

Tyler turned his head a fraction more and found Nick's mouth with his own.

The kiss started off slow and warm, soon passed hot, and exploded into scorching. Their tongues met and tangled, mouths opening wider. Never one to be on the bottom, Tyler rolled Nick off him and arranged himself on top, taking Nick's mouth again and again, holding his head with both hands. He wedged his thigh between Nick's, nudged Nick's cock, and Nick let out a long groan.

"You were horny before we even started this," Nick whispered when Tyler moved his mouth away to rub his jaw against Nick's, to kiss his neck.

"Yeah." Nick knew him better than anyone. Although that comment Kaelin had made earlier had startled him with her scary insight.

"You want her," Nick said, then gasped when Tyler nipped his jaw. "You wanted her then. And you want her now."

"I want you," Tyler growled.

Nick laughed. "I know." He grabbed Tyler's head and kissed him hard. "You're so fucked-up."

"So are you." Tyler reached for Nick's crotch, cupped his junk and squeezed another sharp breath out of him. "Wanna get fucked?"

Chapter Four

Margot and Kaelin sat at the kitchen island drinking coffee the next morning. Margot had slept restlessly and her head throbbed this morning. She rubbed her temples.

"I'm not really into this spa thing," Kaelin said to her. She glanced at her watch. "But Avery wants to do it for us."

"It'll be fun," Margot said with a smile. "Just you girls. And you've worked so hard on the wedding plans, you deserve a day of relaxation. What time is Maddie coming?"

"About ten thirty. Our appointment is at eleven."

Giving in to the pounding at her temples, Margot slid off the stool and moved to a cupboard where she shook a couple of pills out of a bottle and into her hand. She caught Kaelin's eye. "Just a little headache," she said with a smile. She washed the tablets down with coffee.

"I'm sorry again about the scene last night," Kaelin said.

Margot bit her lip, tension zooming back at the memory. She'd so hoped that Tyler's homecoming was going to be a reunion full of hugs and long talks about his life. It hadn't worked out that way. He hadn't even wanted to stay in their home, instead had gotten a hotel room. She'd hidden her deep disappointment with frantic efforts to serve drinks and food and make cheerful small talk with guests. And then Tyler had somehow managed to antagonize sweet little Kaelin.

She and Kaelin had spent a lot of time together the last few months, working on wedding plans, and a connection had built between them, an understanding that Margot suspected was one-sided. Over the years Margot had learned to hide her feelings deep inside her, to keep that careful, perfect façade in place at all times, so it wasn't surprising that Kaelin wouldn't know how she felt, but Kaelin was young and Margot easily recognized that same kind of restless yearning she herself kept hidden. She didn't think anyone else saw that in Kaelin—she was a sweet girl, well liked at the law firm, loved by the seniors she visited with her little dog, regarded with affection by everyone in town. But for both of them, the wedding had been something in their lives out of the ordinary, something they could throw their energy and creativity into.

There was no shortage of money in the Wirth household, something Margot realized she had come to take for granted, especially when she thought the almost unthinkable thought of leaving her husband. She knew she'd tried to go overboard with the wedding plans. Avery was her only daughter, this was the only chance she was ever going to have to do this, and she wanted it to be so special for her baby. Tyler—would Tyler ever marry? The fact that he'd shown up with Nick in tow resurrected all those crazy doubts she'd had years ago. But Avery had invited Nick to the wedding, and he and Tyler were business partners now, so it wasn't incongruous that he would be there too.

"Don't worry about it," she said now to Kaelin, though she felt how tight her lips were as she spoke. "Tyler has this way of getting under people's skin." She immediately felt disloyal, as if she should have defended her son, not blamed him, but Kaelin was sitting right there in front of her, clearly feeling awful about what had happened, and she wanted to make Kaelin feel better.

"That's true," Kaelin said quietly. She stared at her coffee.

Avery burst into the kitchen then, with her usual exuberance. "Oh, coffee, good! I need caffeine." She poured herself a cup. "Isn't Maddie here yet?"

At that moment the front doorbell rang and Avery popped out to answer it.

"Maddie seems very nice," Margot said to Kaelin.

Kaelin gave a small smile. "Yes. She is."

"Well, you girls go and enjoy your day."

"What are you doing today?" Kaelin asked, rising from her stool and heading toward the dishwasher to put away her mug. Warmth expanded in Margot's chest, that Kaelin felt enough at home there to do that. Kaelin hadn't had an easy life, and since her parents had died, Margot had felt almost a responsibility, a maternal need to look after her.

Which was silly, because Kaelin was an adult and capable of looking after herself, but still... Margot knew Kaelin had had to give up hopes and dreams, just as she herself had. When Margot had gotten pregnant at age twenty, had given in to the pressure to marry, which mostly came from Ken, and to drop out of college, her life had changed forever from how she'd always envisioned it, and she knew Kaelin's life, too, wasn't what she'd always thought she'd have. With Margot's own children gone, perhaps it was natural that she'd look for someone else to transfer those maternal feelings to.

Margot smiled. "I have some last-minute things to look after for the rehearsal dinner tonight. Dry cleaning to pick up. A few other errands." Trivial, boring errands, but at least it was something to take up her time until the dinner that evening when once more her family would all be together and they'd have another chance at coming back together as a family.

Tyler and Nick carried boxes of decorations up to the house Kaelin had grown up in, a small white bungalow in a nice neighborhood. Tyler eyed the neatly painted dark green shutters, the bright flowers in the flowerbeds and the grapevine wreath adorning the front door. He rested the box on the railing of the steps and pressed the doorbell. Immediately a dog started barking incessantly from somewhere in the house, the noise getting louder as the animal apparently charged at the door. Tyler lifted a brow at Nick.

A moment later the door opened and Kaelin stood there holding a small black-and white-dog, some sort of terrier mix, Tyler guessed. The dog still barked its head off, but now that he saw it, he was amused at the difference between the ferocious sound of it and the small size of it.

His gaze moved up to Kaelin's face, completely bare of makeup, making her look about fifteen years old, sweet and innocent.

"We brought the decorations," he said. "There are more boxes in the car."

"Oh. Thank you." She stepped aside, the dog still growling at them, so they could carry the boxes in.

"Where do you want them?" Nick asked.

Tyler glanced around at the neat interior with shiny hardwood floors, the modern décor of the living room with funky red leather furniture and stainless steel tables catching his eye. How very un-Kaelin-like. It would be like seeing her in a red leather miniskirt and stilettos.

Which would be extremely hot.

Jesus.

"You can just set them here in the hall," she said. "I'm going to put Taz down, but don't worry, he doesn't bite."

"Like I was worried," Tyler said, dropping the box to the floor. The little dog ran up to him, but now he was free, he became much less aggressive. Tyler bent and held out the back of his fingers for him to sniff. "Hey, pooch." He looked up at Kaelin and realized she was wearing nothing but a silky robe, and he meant *nothing*, because he could clearly see her bare breasts outlined through the thin fabric, her sharp little nipples poking out. His groin tightened and he had to swallow and look back at the dog. "What's his name?"

"Taz."

He scratched Taz's head. Damn, he was pretty cute.

"Why Taz?"

"He does this thing when I get home. He gets so excited he spins around in circles. Like a—"

"Tasmanian Devil."

"Yeah."

She scooped him up again, and Tyler wasn't sure if she was protecting the dog, or hoping the dog would protect her, at least by covering her nearly naked body.

They carried in the other boxes. "You gonna need help with this tomorrow?" Nick asked.

"Oh no, I'll be fine. I have all day to get stuff over to the hotel and pick up the flowers. I'll be fine. Thanks for doing that today."

"How was the spa?" Tyler asked. "All buffed and polished?" And he dragged his gaze down her body. Her cheeks lit on fire.

"I suppose," she said. She held out one hand, her nails all shiny pink with white tips.

"Pretty. Let's see the toes."

Her cheeks got even redder, if possible, but she extended one foot out to show her pink toenails. Her feet were as adorable as the rest of her.

What the fuck was he thinking?

"We gotta go," he muttered, earning a startled glance from Nick. "I need a beer before the rehearsal."

"Okay," she said, still holding that little dog, which was looking up at her adoringly. "See you there."

"I don't want anyone to walk me down the aisle." Avery's voice was low but strained.

"But your father wants to do it," Mrs. Wirth said.

They stood in the hushed vestibule of First Presbyterian Church, an exquisite building of honey-colored stone and stained glass. Kaelin watched Avery and her mother having their low-voiced argument, her hands clasped tightly.

"I've lived on my own for a long time," Avery said through tight lips. "Nobody owns me to give me away. I'm walking down the aisle alone."

"But, Avery—"

"That's it, Mom. Let's get on with it."

Kaelin licked her lips and moved to the door to give the signal to the guitarist and pianist. Avery had eschewed the traditional organ for these two musicians, who began Vivaldi's *Guitar Concerto in D Major*. Maddie started down the aisle, and Kaelin followed her at the appropriate interval.

The rest of the rehearsal went smoothly despite the faint tension buzzing in the air. When they were done, Avery and Scott went and spoke to the musicians while the rest of the group left the sanctuary. Kaelin paused and looked back at Avery. Did she need help with something? Was there a problem with the music? Avery had never decided on a song for the recessional, so maybe that's what they were discussing. Avery caught her eye and waved for Kaelin to go on to the hotel for the dinner.

Throughout dinner, Kaelin's nerves felt stretched taut at the tension that still zinged between Tyler and his parents, and between Tyler and her. Avery chatted brightly and nonstop, fueled by nervous energy and several large glasses of wine, and Kaelin had to make an effort for her sake to keep conversation going, but it was exhausting her.

It would help if Tyler would say more than two words, sitting there grim-faced and silent, drinking red wine. She wanted to kick him under the table, but he was too far away from her and she didn't have the courage to give him hell in front of everyone else. Could she get him out of the room for a minute somehow? She nibbled her bottom lip then remembered that Avery had given her Tyler's cell phone number earlier when he'd been a few minutes late showing up at the church. She'd just started to call him when he'd arrived.

She pulled her phone out of her purse and, holding it on her lap below the table, she thumbed in a message and sent it. "U R acting like an asshole again. Cld U at least pretend U R happy to be here."

His phone must be on vibrate because she didn't hear a thing, but he reached for it on his hip and pulled it out. He read it, read it again, and then his blue gaze zeroed in on her. His mouth twitched.

She lifted her chin and then her wineglass, tilting her head, holding his gaze.

He bent his head and she waited, knowing he was replying.

Her phone vibrated on her lap and she flipped it open discreetly. "I am a dick," she read. Laughter bubbled up in her throat and her fingertips flew to her mouth. "Sorry."

She tightened her lips in to keep her amusement from showing. "Don't think apologizing makes it okay for U to act like a dick," she sent back, a feeling of satisfaction sweeping through her. She could text message him the things she wanted to say but didn't have the nerve.

She shot him a glance as he read her next message, anticipating his response. He read it, sat back in his seat and looked at her again, this time thoughtfully. Oh-oh. Had she pissed him off?

He slid his phone back into the case on his hip, picked up his wineglass, then set it down and reached for the phone again. He was typing in his message, when Avery said, "Tyler. What are you doing?"

He looked up guiltily. "Uh. Sorry." His thumbs made a couple more quick moves and he shoved the phone back on his hip. "A...uh...business call."

Kaelin's phone vibrated again. She glanced around the table to see if anyone was looking at her, but no, everyone was frowning at Tyler. She sighed. She'd gotten him into trouble again, dammit. One handed, she flipped open the phone to read the message. "U R right. Did I tell U how hot U look tonite?"

Heat flooded her, rushing from her chest up over her face to her hairline, all the way down to her toes. When she looked at him, he wasn't looking at her but was smiling wickedly.

She so wanted to message him back, but dammit, she had to stop it. What was he doing, telling her she looked hot?

Just trying to push her buttons, as usual, most likely. He'd always been like that, charming apologies and flattery dripping off his tongue—or thumbs, in this case—to make up for the stupid things he did. And since it always worked for him, he knew he could get away with pretty much anything with anyone. Well, except for his parents.

She swallowed some wine. Well, he couldn't make up for what he'd done to her ten years ago with a cheesy compliment. Sent by text, no less. Geez.

Margot poked at the chicken with prosciutto, rosemary and white wine, her appetite nonexistent. The rehearsal had gone well, although she knew Avery's refusal to let her father walk her down the aisle had disappointed him. She glanced at her husband, talking to Scott's father about the stock market. She suspected the only reason he wanted to walk his daughter down the aisle was so that people would see him doing it, because that's what people expected, and not out of any real sentimental feelings of giving his little girl away. She sighed.

Now Tyler was sitting there, scowling and looking bored and, for god's sake, sending text messages on his cell phone that were apparently business. Then he snapped his phone shut, smiled that devilish charming grin that had gotten him his own way too many times, but that still melted her heart. And he too started talking to his father and Scott's dad about the stock market, sounding impressively knowledgeable.

The stock market was probably the last thing Margot was interested in, but she was happy to sit and listen to her son talk, warmth and pride swelling inside her. And then Scott's dad asked Tyler a question about his business, and she was even more happy to listen to him talk about that, so smart and talented and articulate.

"New platforms—mobile, internet, gaming—are definitely changing the dynamic of the business," Tyler said. "But that just makes it more exciting. Lots more opportunities for creative talent to really stand out."

She almost trembled with maternal pride, smiling and listening.

Soon the dinner was over and it had gone off without a hitch, which of course it would after her careful planning, attention to detail and numerous phone calls to the hotel to check on things. And then she heard Tyler talking about taking Scott and his best man, Hardeep, out somewhere for a drink. Oh dear lord.

Kaelin focused on the dinner conversation again, Tyler now looking interested and actually participating. Apparently Scott wanted to go out with the guys for a last single night and Tyler was agreeing to take him and Hardeep and show them the local watering holes.

Oh dear lord.

Kaelin looked anxiously at Avery, but she was all for it. "That sounds like a great idea!" she said to Tyler. "It would be good for you and Scott to get to know each other better."

"Yeah," he agreed, seeming sincere. "I'll call Nick and see if he wants to come too."

"I don't know," Mrs. Wirth said, a hand at her throat. Her eyes darted around. "That might not be a good idea. You don't want to be tired tomorrow, or..."

"Hungover?" Tyler supplied.

She frowned. "Well, yes."

"Don't worry, Mom, I'll behave. We'll just go have a couple beers somewhere."

Mrs. Wirth chewed on her bottom lip.

"Kaelin and Maddie will come back to our place," Avery said. "And we'll have some girl time."

Kaelin smiled and nodded. "Sure." As if they hadn't had enough girl time earlier that day. But it was Avery and it was Avery's wedding.

Back at the Wirth house, the girls curled up on couches and chairs in the family room with more wine. Well, Maddie and Avery had more wine, Kaelin had had enough, and she had to drive back to her place. It wasn't long before Maddie and Avery started talking and laughing about things that had happened and people Kaelin didn't know. She tried to smile and look interested, but that left-out feeling swept over her.

"Hey," Avery said to Kaelin. "When are you going to come visit me in Los Angeles again?"

Kaelin smiled. "Well, obviously not right away. You're leaving on your honeymoon tomorrow night."

"You should move there, Kaelin." Avery sat up and leaned forward. "Seriously. I miss you so much. We could have so much fun living in the same city again."

"I can't move, Ave, you know that."

"Why not?" Avery's full lips pouted a bit.

"My whole life is here." Kaelin gave her a crooked smile and lifted one shoulder. "My job. My family. My house."

"Your only family here is your Aunt Lara. Your cousins have left. Your parents are gone. And with your experience, you could easily get a job at a law firm in L.A."

"I have Taz," she added feebly. "I can't move to an apartment with him, and I'm sure I'd never be able to afford a house in Los Angeles."

They'd had this conversation before, but the last time Kaelin had genuinely dismissed the idea. Now, though, she actually let herself think about it. But just for a minute. Leaving everything she knew, everything that was safe and secure and stable, to move across the country to a strange city where she knew no one—that was terrifying.

But once again, that feeling of vague dissatisfaction nudged her. She wasn't close with Aunt Lara. Her job was fine. She enjoyed it. She had friends in Mapleglen. But not close friends. Her best friends had moved away, all over the country. And her relationship with Brent hadn't worked out so well. Her insides twisted a little thinking of what she'd wanted from him but had been too afraid to ask for.

She was safe here. Better to stay with what she had and what she knew than to risk it all by leaving.

She shook her head, still with that smile pasted firmly in place. "Well, you never know," she said. "Maybe someday."

Avery's eyes widened. "Well, at least that's not an out-and-out no. You know I'd love it if you moved closer."

"I'd like to be closer," Kaelin admitted. Though she wasn't sure how well she'd fit into Avery's new world. She and Scott, and Hardeep and Maddie, formed a neat little foursome and she'd be a…what? A fifth wheel?

"Think about it," Avery urged her. "I know it's a big decision. I'm not saying quit your job tomorrow. But think about it."

And Kaelin found herself agreeing to that, although she suspected it was mostly just to keep Avery happy. She couldn't seriously think about doing something so life-altering.

"So tomorrow, what time will you come over, Kaelin? To get ready."

"I don't know. I have lots to do tomorrow. We have to decorate, pick up flowers, and make sure the cupcakes are delivered and—"

"I'll help," Maddie said.

"I will too," Avery added.

"No, you don't have to." Kaelin smiled. "You're the bride."

"Thank you, Kaelin. You've been so sweet about all this."

58

Kaelin just shrugged and smiled, uncomfortable with the praise.

They planned the schedule for the next day. The ceremony was at four o'clock. Kaelin knew she could not get into the hotel ballroom where the reception was being held until noon, so she could pick up the flowers in the morning and bring them to the Wirth house. There were also decorations for the church, and she had to make sure the flowers were delivered there and arranged properly.

A few hours later, Maddie left to go back to the hotel where she and Hardeep were staying and Kaelin smothered a yawn. "I should go too," she said just as Avery's cell phone buzzed.

Avery set down her wine and picked it up. "Hi, hon," she said, surprise tingeing her voice. Then she frowned. "What?" Her voice changed to sharp. "Are you serious?" Then Avery bit her lip and glanced at her mother. "Oh, honey, okay," she said, smiling, but Kaelin could see how tight that smile was. "Um...okay, we'll be there in a little bit." She listened, her eyebrows drawing down and her eyes flickering. "Yes. Yes. Got it. Okay, bye."

She closed her phone, still smiling toothily. "Kaelin, hon, are you okay to drive?"

"Yeah. Of course."

"The guys want us to join them for a drink."

Now it was Kaelin's turn to frown. "You're kidding. Now?"

"Yes. Come on." She grabbed Kaelin's hand and yanked her up off the couch. Kaelin stumbled a little and scurried after Avery's long strides.

"Avery!" her mother called. "Where are you going?"

"Just out for a drink," Avery snapped over her shoulder. "Don't worry, Mom, won't be late. You go on to bed. It's a big day tomorrow."

Kaelin grabbed her purse and Avery hustled her out the front door. Her car was parked on the street and she dug for her keys in her purse. "What's going on?" she asked.

"Hold on. Get in the car." Avery's voice was tight.

Kaelin started the car and put it into gear. "Where are we going?"

"To the police station. Scott's in jail."

Chapter Five

Margot washed her face and brushed out her hair, looking at herself in the mirror. Without her makeup she looked washed-out and tired. She clicked off the light of the ensuite bathroom and moved into the bedroom where Ken lay, reading a magazine.

"The dinner was nice," he said, as usual not effusive with his praise.

"Thank you." She climbed under the covers.

"And you looked beautiful."

Her head whipped to the side to stare at Ken. "Ah...thank you."

He laid down the magazine and closed his eyes. "Margot."

"Yes?" Her heart stuttered.

"I don't want you to leave me."

Pressure built in her chest and her eyes ached. "I don't want to leave you. But I can't go on like this."

"But why? I don't understand...you have the perfect life. You can do whatever you want to do..."

"I can't do whatever I want!" Outrage had her sitting up straight, staring at him. "Are you kidding me? Our whole life is what *you* want me to do! *You* want me to belong to the country club, to associate with the wives of the other doctors, to host dinner parties. You want me to do charity work, and not that I begrudge the children's ward at the hospital one moment of my time or one cent that we've raised, but that's what *you* want! When I want to go to the carnival, we can't because it's not done. When I want to drive around to the wineries in the hills and taste wine, we can't do that because it's too touristy. When I want to go for a walk on the beach in the moonlight, we can't because you have to get up early the next morning. When I want to travel, we can't because you can't take time off work. I can't do anything I want!"

He opened his eyes and stared back at her, eyebrows drawn down.

"And on top of that, you don't even want me anymore," she cried, fingers curling into fists. "I try so hard to stay in shape, to look nice for you, and you don't even care!"

She almost felt sorry for him at how shocked and uncomfortable he looked at her outburst. "I...I do care."

She remembered his compliment from moments ago, not the first he'd ever given her but the first in a long time.

"You care because you want me to look good so you look good!"

"That's not true."

"It is true. Don't deny it."

He closed his eyes. He couldn't deny it. It was true.

"But I do still care about you," he said. "I love you, Margot."

Her eyes stung and she blinked at him through a blur of tears. "Oh, Ken." He reached for her then, and she fell against him, tears falling. "I love you too. I do. But I need more."

He tipped her face up and kissed her mouth, once, twice, then longer, deeper. She sank into the kiss, slid her arms around his neck and kissed him back. She still loved the feel of his arms around her, strong and warm. A tingling started down low inside her, quickly turning into a sharp ache of desire. She still loved him.

His hands moved on her body, sensitizing her skin, her breasts.

"You are beautiful," he murmured against her mouth. "Margot. We'll figure this all out."

At that moment, she thought maybe they could. He rolled her to her back and moved over her, heavy and warm on top of her, solid and reassuring as they made love. It was familiar but still hot, comfortable but still exciting. He knew just how to make her come, and she writhed beneath him as pleasure rippled through her, held him tightly through his own release. These moments of closeness were what gave her hope, what made her think they could get through this. They'd had marital problems before—what couple didn't?—and if it hadn't been for their physical intimacy, she wasn't sure they would have made it. Maybe they'd make it this time too.

When she'd been twenty years old, pregnant and scared, he'd seemed so mature, so responsible, like someone who would take care of her forever. And he had, in so many ways. Why did she want more? Was there something wrong with her, that this life of money and privilege wasn't enough for her?

"I love you, Ken," she whispered.

"I love you too."

"I know I've been stressed about the wedding. And about Tyler coming home."

"It's okay."

"I was so looking forward to seeing him," she murmured, her fingers rubbing over Ken's shoulder. "But he hasn't even wanted to talk to me."

Ken was silent. No, he wouldn't talk about it. She knew it. She swallowed a sob, her disappointment at how things were going with Tyler almost choking her. Tomorrow was the wedding. It was probably her last chance to try to connect with Tyler, to tell him how she felt, if he'd even bother to talk to her. The next day he would leave again, and what would happen after that?

For some reason, the wedding and making things up with Tyler had gotten all twisted up in her mind with making a new start, with things being better, with the rest of her life being different, and she had a dismal, creeping feeling that it wasn't going to work out that way. Tyler wanted nothing to do with her, and Avery was getting married and going back to Los Angeles, and the rest of Margot's life stretched out in front of her empty and barren and terrifying.

Tyler sat in the Mapleglen police station, head in his hands. Somehow he just knew this was going to end up his fault. Meanwhile he had a black eye and the groom was in a holding cell. Christ.

He hadn't wanted Scott to call Avery. He was sure they could have figured out a way out of this without his sister ever having to know her future husband had been stupid drunk and gotten his ass arrested. Now she was on her way there and oh man, there was going to be shit hitting the fan. He groaned.

Hardeep let out a snore, passed out in the chair next to him. Nick's hand rubbed Tyler's back, but just briefly. And then Avery came tearing in, all outraged blonde hair and blue eyes. Kaelin was right behind her. Shit.

Tyler surged to his feet and met his sister.

"Where the hell is he?" she demanded. "And what the fuck

is going on?"

"Sshh, calm down," he said, taking her hands. "He's fine."

She snorted. "He may be fine now, but just wait. Jesus Christ, what the hell were you guys doing, Tyler?"

"Well, um. We went to Fitzgeralds. 'Cause, you know, you have to go there when you come to Mapleglen."

She glared at him.

"He had a few shots of Jameson. A couple of Guinness. Then he wanted to go somewhere with...uh..." He shot Nick a pleading glance. Nick sat back, arms folded across his chest, very unhelpfully. "Uh, more action," he finished, euphemistically

But Avery wasn't stupid. "Christ," she said. "You took him to the Pussy Cat Palace, didn't you?"

Tyler grimaced. "Uh. Yeah. It's totally my fault, I should never have told him about the place."

Avery's eyes shot blue sparks. "No shit."

"He said you don't mind when he goes to see exotic dancers."

Avery's lips compressed. "Whatever. So how did he get arrested?"

Tyler looked at Kaelin. Her pretty face was expressionless. She was probably as pissed at him as Avery was, but she was trying hard not to show it. "Well. When we left, we were waiting for a taxi, and down the street from the Pussy Palace, I mean Pussy Cat Palace, there was a fire truck parked on the street. Didn't seem to be a fire, and all the firefighters were inside somewhere, but Scott said...uh...he'd always wanted to be a firefighter. He said you have a thing for firefighters, in their uniforms, and you guys do this role play thing..."

Avery's face went scarlet. Well shit, sharing that might have been a mistake.

"Anyway," he hurried on, glancing at Kaelin, whose lips twitched. "He climbed up into the fire truck. I tried to stop him, Ave, I swear it. I grabbed his shirt—um, that's why it's ripped— and tried to pull him down but he was determined. And then...well..." He paused. He wasn't doing a good job of this. Avery looked more and more furious with every word. Maybe there wasn't going to be a wedding tomorrow.

"So." He grinned. "We all got in and then I saw the keys were in the vehicle and I thought, hey, might as well make his last single night one to remember and I started the truck up and we went for a ride."

Silence expanded thickly around them all in the waiting room, other than the small choking noise Nick made.

"You...you..." Avery stared at him, mouth gaping. *"You went for a ride? In a fire truck?"*

He lifted his shoulders.

"Are you fucking insane?" she yelled, and the officer on duty at the desk looked up and frowned. She punched Tyler's chest and he jumped. "What the hell were you thinking? And why aren't you the one arrested?"

"Uh. Little mix-up. When the cops caught us. They thought Scott was driving, but he wasn't. I tried to tell them, but...you know." He made a face and lifted his hands. "Cops. I'm really sorry, Ave. But we'll get him out. It's just a misunderstanding."

He looked at Kaelin, whose eyes were closed, her lips trembling. Hell, she was *laughing*. What the fuck?

"What do we have to do?" Avery demanded. "To get him out?"

"They said we can...uh...post bail. But not until tomorrow."

Avery's screech had him wincing.

Kaelin went over to the desk. "Hi, Officer Cuthbert," she said. "Is Brent working tonight?"

"Hey, Kaelin. No he's not."

"Okay. Thanks."

Kaelin pulled her cell phone out of her purse and punched in a number. She waited. Who the hell was she calling?

"Hi, Brent," she said. "It's me, Kaelin. Yeah. Good. Um...I have a little problem."

She turned away and walked to the end of the waiting room so Tyler couldn't hear her. Shit. She was talking to the cop boyfriend. Or whatever he was to her. She said they'd broken up. A moment later she returned, off the phone.

"Brent's coming," she told Avery, patting her shoulder. "We'll get this all sorted out."

Tyler scowled at her and she blinked at him.

"Can I see him?" Avery demanded.

"Sure," the officer on duty said. "We'll bring him to a room. Be about ten minutes."

"Ten..." She looked like she was going to explode. "Fine." She stomped over to the chair and sat down, casting Hardeep a baleful look.

She set her purse on her lap and folded her hands over it, staring resolutely across the room.

"It'll be okay, Avery." Kaelin sat beside her and rubbed her shoulder. "It's not that big a deal."

Now it was Tyler's turn to gape at her. Scott was in jail. He'd stolen a fucking fire truck. And it was no big deal? To the girl who followed all the rules, played it safe, never drew attention to herself?

Tyler slumped down into one of the cheap plastic chairs. He'd been to this police station years ago under similar circumstances. He and Nick had taken Nick's grandma's car for a joy ride when they'd been fifteen, and not only got caught, but had been caught with beer in the car. His parents had been unfuckingbelievably pissed off when they'd come to get him that night. Then there was the time Dad's car had been totaled. And then, that incident ten years ago. He'd been so shit scared that he was going to end up in jail again, only that time he was nearly an adult and... He shook his head, blocking that gut-wrenching memory.

Moments later, a man walked into the station, tall, broad, short-cropped dark hair, square jaw. Tyler wanted to punch him the minute he saw him, knowing exactly who it was. The guy went straight to Kaelin.

"Kaelin, honey, what's going on?"

She rose, gave him a hesitant smile and let him hug her. Tyler's gut twisted and his skin tightened, and he scowled at them. Kaelin explained the situation to the guy, introduced him briefly to the others, Hardeep still snoring away. Then Cop Boy nodded and disappeared through a door. Kaelin met his hard stare.

"What?" she asked.

"That's the boyfriend?"

"Um...ex. Sort of."

Sort of? What the hell did that mean?

"You said you broke up."

"Yes." She nibbled her bottom lip as she took her seat again, perching on the edge of the chair. "We did. He still wants to get back together. I guess."

"You guess?" *Fuck.*

"Okay, he does. But you know. It didn't work out, so..." Her voice trailed off.

"Sucked in bed, huh?"

Her eyes shot wide. "Tyler!"

He laughed. Her expression said it all. It was true. Man, he could show her. Cop Boy didn't know how to satisfy her, but he could.

Christ. He was drunk.

He had to be shitfaced to be thinking things like that. He slumped lower in the chair. His shiner throbbed and his shoulder twinged a little from the tussle he'd had with Scott. Hell. Shit. Fuck. Damn.

It wasn't long before Scott appeared, looking like crap, what little hair he had mussed, his eyes red, shirt ripped. Cop Boy was behind him. Avery jumped to her feet and rushed toward Scott, and Kaelin rose too, slower, and moved toward Brent.

Tyler watched glumly, though relief slid through him that Scott was out. Reluctant gratitude toward Cop Boy rose inside him. He stood.

"Thank you so much," Kaelin said breathlessly, gripping Cop Boy's big biceps. Tyler gritted his teeth. "I so much appreciate this, Brent."

"Not a problem. You know I'd do anything for you. And I'm sure this was all just a misunderstanding."

"Thank you." Avery turned to him as well. She eyed him up and down, glanced at Kaelin then back at Brent. "Thank you so much, Brent. We're getting married tomorrow."

"I know." Brent grinned. "Take your fiancé home and put him to bed so he's not too hungover to say his vows tomorrow."

Shit. The guy was decent. But when Brent looked down at Kaelin, standing beside him in her sexy little black dress and heels, Tyler saw the hunger in his eyes and once again wanted to deck the sonofabitch. His hands curled into fists.

"I'm driving," Kaelin said. "I'll take you home first, Avery, and then I'll take the guys back to the hotel." Scott had a room there too.

They woke Hardeep and dragged him out of the station. Scott wasn't all that steady either, so it took Nick to help Hardeep and Tyler to help Scott. Then they discovered there were only three seatbelts in the back seat of Kaelin's little black Mazda.

She stood there biting her lip.

"Oh for Chrissake," Tyler said. "We've already been arrested once tonight, it won't happen again."

"What if I get in an accident?" She turned big brown eyes on him. "I don't want anyone killed before the wedding."

"But after the wedding is okay," Avery said, and Hardeep cracked up laughing and almost fell over.

Kaelin rolled her eyes. "Get in," she said, climbing into the driver's seat. "But if I get a ticket, you guys will all be sorry."

"Just get Cop Boy to cancel it," Tyler suggested, shoving Scott into the back seat.

Scott grunted and fell in. With Nick, Scott and Hardeep all in, Avery climbed in and arranged herself over their laps. Jesus, it was like high school all over again, breaking the rules, drinking and driving, not wearing seatbelts. Tyler sighed. Somehow it wasn't as much fun as it had been then.

Kaelin drove through dark quiet streets to the Wirth home and Tyler recognized that she was staying off main streets and taking a zigzag route. He smiled at her with admiration from his place in the front passenger seat and patted her thigh approvingly. She smacked his hand away.

"What?" He turned hurt eyes on her. "You're doing good, sweetheart."

She shot him a glance, mouth tight, hands on the steering wheel.

Avery climbed out when they got to their parents' place. She gripped the edge of the open passenger door window, bent down and glared at Tyler. "Make sure he gets back to the hotel safe and sound," she snapped. "So I can kick his ass tomorrow when he can feel it."

Tyler winced. "Avery, remember, this was my fault? He just wanted to look at the truck."

"No way, man," Scott piped up from the back seat. "I wanted to drive that fucker!"

Avery's gaze shifted behind Tyler to stare at Scott. "Uh huh," she said. "All right, then." She looked back at Tyler, and her eyes narrowed. Then her gaze softened and her mouth twisted. "Tyler."

"What? Seriously, Ave, don't be mad at him." He patted one of her hands. "He's drunk."

"I know." She sighed. "So are you." She bent lower to peer at Kaelin. "You okay, hon? To take them to the hotel?"

"I'm fine. You go in and get your beauty sleep for tomorrow."

Avery looked back at Tyler with a fierce expression on her face. "Mom and Dad know nothing about this. Right?"

Tyler nearly choked. Oh hell yeah. "Right." He held up a hand. "Absolutely."

Avery walked up the front sidewalk. Kaelin waited until Avery was inside the house then pulled out. She drove to the hotel, this time heading onto Main Street and down toward the river where the Red Maple Inn was located.

Tyler chewed on the inside of his mouth as he debated what to say. He turned around to look at the guys in the back seat. Hardeep was snoring again, and Scott's head was back, eyes closed, mouth open. Tyler met Nick's amused eyes. Nick quirked an eyebrow. Tyler grimaced and turned back to face forward.

"Thanks for coming," he said to Kaelin quietly.

She nodded, eyes forward.

"And thanks for helping." He didn't even want to mention Cop Boy.

Her chin lifted. "You're welcome."

He searched around in his brain for something else to say. He remembered their text messages during the dinner, his astonishment that she'd told him he was acting like an asshole. Only Nick ever told him stuff like that and got away with it. "You really do look hot tonight."

She turned and leveled him with a scorching look, then resumed her eyes-forward driving.

Damn, she was pretty. Her small nose created a sweet profile, her little chin lifted, her long eyelashes fluttering as she watched the road. She parked in the lot of the hotel, and between the three of them, they managed to drag Scott and Hardeep out of the car and get them awake enough to walk through the lobby. At this late hour, few people were around other than the staff at the front desk. They rode the elevator to the third floor where Hardeep's and Scott's rooms were. They got Hardeep safely inside and face-down on his bed next to a sleeping Maddie, then Scott to his room, which was the honeymoon suite where he and Avery would stay the next night after the wedding.

"Are you going to be okay?" Kaelin asked Scott, worry creasing her forehead.

"Yeah, yeah," he said. He aimed a kiss at her forehead and ended up bumping her temple, then started taking off his clothes. Tyler frowned and set his hands on Kaelin's small shoulders, turning her away from Scott and toward the door.

"I'm in room 405," he told Scott. "Call if you need anything."

"Sure, man, thanks. Sorry about tonight."

"Don't apologize to me. Save that for Avery tomorrow." He was going to need to suck up big time. Hoo boy.

They left Scott in his room, and Nick and Tyler rode down the elevator with Kaelin and strolled across the empty lobby with her. Tyler stopped in front of one of the couches arranged around the fireplace, still burning with a warm glow, and pulled Kaelin down to sit beside him.

Nick paused, looked at him, then sat down too, on the other side of her.

Tyler blew out a long breath. "Wow. That turned out to be a crazy night." He leaned back into the couch.

"No kidding," Kaelin said. "I can't believe that happened."

"Thank you again, Kaelin." Tyler took her hand.

After a short pause, she said, "It wasn't your fault, was it?"

"I am fully willing to take the blame if it will save Scott's ass," Tyler said carefully. He shot her a wary glance. She smiled. Such a sweet smile, the curve of her mouth so appealing.

"Trouble just seems to follow you around."

Nick laughed and she turned to look at him. Tyler watched them, the wordless connection between them, watched as Nick took her other hand and gave it a gentle squeeze.

Something shifted inside Tyler. It wasn't jealousy. He *liked* it that they liked each other. He always had. In some ways, Nick and Kaelin were so much alike—steady, dependable. So unlike him. Probably Cop Boy was like that too—he was an officer of the law. He had to be serious and responsible too. Irritation rubbed inside Tyler.

Okay, *that* was jealousy.

Thinking about Kaelin with that guy bugged the hell out of him.

"How's your eye, bud?" Nick asked him.

He focused his attention back on Kaelin and Nick, now both looking at him.

"I'm okay."

"What happened?" Kaelin waited for his response, eyes clear, not judgmental or critical.

He rolled his eyes. "I tried to stop Scott from getting in the fire truck. He got a little carried away and accidentally knocked his elbow into my eye."

Kaelin licked her lips, her little tongue dragging over the bottom lip in a gesture so sexy Tyler's body heated.

"Oh, Tyler. Were you really trying to stop him?"

One corner of his mouth kicked up. "Yeah. I really was."

"He really was," Nick added.

She slowly shook her head from side to side.

Thick heat built around them, and his heart started thudding in his chest. He felt like his lungs were burning when he dragged air into them and there was no way he could resist touching her, her silky hair, the soft skin of her cheek and jaw, his thumb trailing over her velvety bottom lip.

Their eyes met and held in a stretched-out connection.

She didn't move away from his touch, although she was sitting with both her hands captured by his and Nick's, sandwiched between them, but she wasn't trying to get away, and he let his hand drift to her shoulder.

"You're so sweet, Kaelin," he said hoarsely. "You put the whole wedding together for Avery. You bailed out Scott. Even my mom loves you."

A tiny huff of laughter escaped her at that.

Tyler looked at Nick, who also gazed at Kaelin's face with a look of admiration and yes, hunger.

Nick wanted her too.

As if sensing Tyler's gaze on him, Nick looked away from Kaelin, and his and Tyler's gazes locked. Unspoken questions passed between them.

Tyler closed his eyes. It was futile to even let ideas like that tease the edges of his mind. Kaelin was a good girl, the best kind of good girl, sweet and innocent and no doubt as vanilla as soft-serve ice cream. He'd had to take drastic measures the last time he'd started having outrageous, inappropriate thoughts like that about her, and this could be no different.

"What's wrong?" she whispered, big brown eyes focused on him when he opened his.

His mouth twisted. "Nothing." He lifted the hand he still held and kissed her fingers. Her pupils went wide, eyes dark as she watched him. Hell. "You're just so nice, Kaelin. Such a good girl."

She went very still, sitting there on the couch between him and Nick.

"Really," he continued. "Brent seemed like a nice guy too. You'd make a good couple."

"Oh for Chrissakes!" The words exploded out of her mouth and she yanked her hands out of their grip. "I'm not that nice!"

And she grabbed Tyler's head, yanked him toward her and kissed him hard.

Too stunned to even kiss her back, his head reeled as she

shoved him away, but that was nothing compared to the bolt of lightning that struck him when she turned to Nick, grabbed him and kissed him too.

Chapter Six

Kaelin dragged air into her lungs, her heart racing, her skin hot. Pressure inside her made her feel as if she was going to explode, burst right out of her skin. She was so goddamn *sick* of hearing what a good girl she was.

"I'm not that good," she said, panting as she looked from Nick to Tyler. Their faces wore identical expressions of shocked arousal. She knew they were attracted to her. Of course, she knew! She'd known from the moment she walked into the Wirth home yesterday and their eyes had met. She'd known ten years ago.

Ten years ago she'd had fantasies about Nick and Tyler that she'd admitted to no one, barely even to herself. After that day she'd seen them naked together with another girl, those fantasies had taken on a new life, become even wilder. Where before she'd had dreams of being with them one at a time, after that she had shocking, wicked dreams of being with them both. At the same time. Fantasies she'd never in a million years act on, because...dear lord, they were bad, so bad, and she was a good girl.

She was sick of being a good girl. Sick of being the dutiful daughter who looked after her poor brain-injured dad, who gave up her dreams to come home and care for him when her mom died, who volunteered to work at charity events, who organized a wedding for her best friend, who did everything for everyone else and never for herself.

She wanted so much to be bad, just once, just one incredible wild time, to see what it felt like, to know if that's what was missing from her life.

And what could be badder than a threesome with two sexy guys?

"Kaelin," Tyler's voice rasped. "What the hell."

She slid her arm around his neck and pulled him to her again, kissed him again, and this time he kissed her back, his mouth so hot and delicious, opening wide on hers, his tongue sliding in, stroking over hers. She moaned, let her fingers slide into his hair, holding the back of his skull, so big and solid. Tyler's body radiated heat and a fine trembling and she longed to climb onto him and press up against him, her breasts aching, her pussy throbbing.

Nick's body on the other side of her was even bigger and just as hot, burning against her hip and she dragged her mouth away from Tyler's and turned back to him. She met his eyes, his silvery-gray eyes usually cool and calm, now blazing with heat. It was different with him, she couldn't say exactly comfortable, because she still felt that ache, that flutter low down inside, but it wasn't as intense and scary as with Tyler.

And when she leaned toward him, he lifted a hand and cupped her cheek, his mouth on hers not as demanding, gentler and slower, his lips not as full. She moaned softly, heard Tyler's sharply drawn breath, felt his excitement as much as she felt Nick's.

"Fuck," Tyler whispered beside her. "Kaelin, what the fuck are you doing?"

Power rushed through her like an electrical surge and she pulled away from Nick and smiled.

"I want to be bad," she said.

"What are you saying?" Desperation edged Tyler's voice. His eyes looked searchingly into hers. "Christ, Kaelin, I thought you were the sober one."

"I am sober."

"You can't do this, sweetheart." He closed his eyes and looked as if someone had kneed him the nuts.

"Why not?" Her insides tightened. He wasn't going to turn her down, was he? She was going way out on a limb here, she knew it, risking a lot, something she never, ever did, and if they rejected her, she wasn't sure she'd survive the humiliation. "I know what I'm doing."

"Fuck," he groaned again and looked at Nick pleadingly.

"Kaelin," Nick began, but she cut him off before he could be all rational and sane and talk her out of it.

"You've done it before," she said challengingly. She looked back and forth between them as if daring them to deny it. And how could they? They all knew what had happened that night and what she'd seen.

"Oh Jesus." Tyler looked as if he was in even more pain.

"Well, you have, haven't you? You can't deny it. I saw you. And that's not the only time you've ever done that." She paused. "Is it?"

Nick and Tyler looked at each other again.

"That's not the point, honey," Nick said, his voice gentle. He stroked her shoulder. "This is about you."

"Yes! Exactly!" She sat up straighter. "This is about me! And I want this."

"Both of us," Tyler spoke.

"Yes." She again looked back and forth between them, uncertainty starting to get the better of her, rising up inside her, overpowering this uncharacteristic recklessness. She fought it down, swallowed hard. "Yes."

Tyler glanced around the empty lobby. "This probably isn't the place for this conversation."

Were they going to send her home? She gazed anxiously at them, arousal and excitement tangling with fear and caution.

Again Tyler and Nick shared a glance and she saw understanding pass between them.

"We'll go up to our room," Nick said, standing. He held out a hand and pulled her up, and Tyler rose too.

"You're sharing a room?" she asked, walking across the carpeted lobby between them.

"Yeah."

Okay. Whatever. She was pretty sure Avery had told her they shared an apartment in Chicago. They rode in silence up the elevator again, this time electricity sizzling in the air instead of alcohol fumes. Tyler pulled his wallet out and fished out the keycard, opened the door and let Kaelin precede him into the room.

They'd left a lamp on, a floor lamp by the desk. The rooms in the Red Maple Inn were nice, the nicest hotel in Mapleglen, but nothing special, so she didn't pay much attention to the room or the décor, just clasped her shaking hands together and turned to face the two men.

She must have gone insane. How else could she explain this? She couldn't blame intoxication—she'd only had a couple of glasses of wine at dinner, hours ago. Perhaps a mini stroke? Something that had damaged her frontal lobe or whatever, the part of her brain that knew right from wrong, good from bad, the part that controlled inhibition, like what had happened with her dad.

They stood there looking at her as if she were a bomb about to explode, sending each other sideways glances. They wanted it too, they had to, or they would have hustled her out the front door of the hotel. But they were being...gentlemen.

A smile tugged her lips. Never in a million years would she have thought to use that word to describe Tyler. Badass, troublemaker, devil—never a gentleman.

And yet, it didn't seem inappropriate. He'd pushed her buttons, teased her and tormented her, but he'd never done anything to her that would make her truly fear him. The fear she felt was of her own reactions to him, the way he made her feel—inadequate, unsophisticated...aroused.

"What's so funny?" Tyler demanded hoarsely.

"You are."

He lifted one eyebrow, clearly unused to being the object of amusement.

"I thought you were such a bad boy," she continued, moving toward them where they stood side by side. "What are you afraid of?"

He shook his head, a reluctant smile tipping up the corners of his mouth. His beautiful, sexy mouth. She wanted to lick his mouth. "That won't work, sweetheart."

Her own smile deepened. "I'm not trying to manipulate you."

"Yes, you are. I'm just not sure why. Or where this is coming from. Or what happened to the real Kaelin Daume."

She gave a soft laugh and came to a stop just in front of them. She laid a hand on Tyler's chest and one on Nick's. Nick covered her hand with his, Tyler reached out and rested a hand on her hip.

"I want one night of bad," she said. "Is that so hard to

understand?" She looked from Nick to Tyler. "You guys are leaving on Sunday. I have to stay here in Mapleglen for the rest of my life. Nothing like this will ever happen to me again."

She saw the surrender in Tyler's eyes, followed immediately by a flare of heat.

"Are you sure, Kaelin?" Nick asked quietly.

She held his gaze and nodded.

"Because we're both too horny to say no to you," Nick continued wryly, moving around behind her. "But *you* can stop this any time." She held his gaze, turning to look over her shoulder as he moved. He set his hands on her waist and bent to rub his face on her hair. "Any time. Just say no. Right, Tyler?"

"Right." The word sounded strangled.

"I trust you both," she said. "There's no one else I'd do this with."

Tyler snorted and moved closer, pressing his hips against her. Pressing his erection against her. "You got that right," he said enigmatically. What did that mean? But her thought got lost as he bent his head to kiss her again, heat washing through her like a molten river, and her head went empty as she turned herself over to sensation.

Nick pressed against her back, against her ass, hands on her hips, pulling her back against him, his mouth seeking and finding the side of her neck. His lips and his breath sent shivers cascading over her skin. Nerves had her shaking inside, excitement swelled up huge and potent. And Tyler kissed her mouth.

She'd grabbed him and kissed him earlier but she'd been so incensed and frustrated, she hadn't had time to really enjoy it. The second kiss had been better. But this one...this time she lost herself in it, her hands on Tyler's shoulders, all big bones and muscles, his tongue sliding into her mouth again and again in an erotic rhythm that had her blood pounding through her veins. His thumb on her chin pressed her mouth open wider for him, and she moaned as she opened to him, tasted him.

Crazy, crazy, crazy. The word ran through her mind until it didn't mean anything anymore. Heat flashed over her, her pussy ached with a sharp, hard need, her breasts swelled and Tyler pressed closer, giving them that pressure they needed. Pressed between two big, hard male bodies, her knees went soft and she started to slide down. They both held her up, Tyler's mouth leaving hers.

"I got her," Nick murmured, and bent to slide an arm beneath her knees, scooping her into his arms. She grabbed his shoulder, stared up at him, her pulse beating so hard that was all she could hear, her body burning up with fever.

"I can't fucking believe this," Tyler muttered, striding to the bed and yanking back the covers.

A bed. Was she really going to do this? It was so wanton and wicked and outrageous. More of that old caution and uncertainty slammed into her and the fingers digging into Nick's shoulder trembled. She bit her lip, looking up at him through her eyelashes. When he laid her on the bed, she immediately sat up.

"I...uh..."

"Changed your mind?" Tyler asked.

"No. I mean, I'm not sure."

He sat beside her. The skin on his face stretched taut, he nonetheless took her hand gently. "Kaelin. What do you want to do?"

"I want...I want you to do what you did to Tracy."

When his face changed expression and blanched, she

blinked. And blinked again. And glanced at Nick. Nick frowned. "What do you mean, Kaelin?"

"I mean...I saw you. You tied her up."

Tyler stared at her wordlessly then gave a jerky nod.

"I want you to tie me up," she whispered. She'd never in her entire life voiced that fantasy aloud, though so many times she'd wanted to ask Brent. Every time she saw his handcuffs, her tummy did a little flip of excitement, but she'd never ever had the nerve to tell him that. Somehow she knew Brent was so by the book, follow the rules, he would have been appalled at that idea.

"You want us to tie you up," Tyler repeated. Color washed back into his cheeks, over his high cheekbones, and his eyes glittered. He looked at Nick.

"Yes."

She clasped her hands and bent her head, letting her hair fall over her face. How could she explain this to them? She didn't even know why she wanted it, except that the idea made her hot, so hot, and the idea of having control taken away from her only added to the fire burning inside her.

"I got nothing," Tyler said to Nick, and she peeked through her curtain of hair to see his mouth almost smiling. "Didn't expect this."

"Here." Nick walked to the closet near the door and returned with two silk neckties. Kaelin blinked. "I brought these for the wedding. Wasn't sure which I'd wear."

"Christ," Tyler muttered. He took a tie from Nick and in seconds Kaelin was flat on her back, hands tied to the headboard of the bed above her head.

She stared at him mutely. He was so beautiful. His dark gold hair gleamed in the lamplight, as did the scruff of whiskers on his jaw. His lips parted and he gazed down at her, eyes shining. He smiled at her, and everything inside her tightened. "Do you trust us, Kaelin?"

She nodded. Why she trusted him, she had no idea. Yes, he'd hurt her. He'd kissed her, gotten her young hopes up and then had smashed them to pieces. She'd felt Nick's betrayal too, that he'd been involved in something like that. But at this moment, in this room, she trusted both of them to look after her, and even though the fact that she was helpless and pretty much at their mercy added an edge of thrill to the excitement pounding inside her, she knew they wouldn't abuse that power with her.

"Yes," she whispered, holding Tyler's gaze. "I trust you."

He closed his eyes briefly and then started unbuttoning his shirt. Her eyes widened as she watched his body appear, his broad chest with sculpted muscles, a fine dust of light hair, defined abs. His shoulders shone in the light as he shrugged out of the shirt and it drifted to the floor. When his fingers went to the button of his pants, her mouth went dry, and her pussy clenched. She watched with fascination and admiration as he stepped out of pants and socks, wearing nothing but a tiny pair of snug black boxer briefs that strained to cover his massive erection.

Her eyes turned to Nick who was also undressing, revealing his heavily muscled body, a darker hue than Tyler's golden skin, darker hair dusting his pecs and ripped abs. Oh yes, he had been working out. Definitely.

They both kept their underwear on as they climbed onto the bed, one on either side of her and slowly, carefully began to remove her clothes. Her skin burned and tingled, her breath going short and choppy. Tyler's fingers on the zipper of her dress were slightly unsteady. Nick's hands were warm as he slid them up her bare legs beneath the dress. He stroked her thighs and she could only tremble and stare at both of them wide eyed, arms stretched above her head.

"Gonna have to untie you," Tyler muttered, reaching for the silk ties. He loosened her arms and lowered them to her sides. When he slowly slid the wide straps of her sleeveless dress down her arms, her tummy muscles clenched hard and she shivered. Her breasts swelled in the cups of her strapless black bra, nipples tingling. She watched him watch her, loved how his eyes got so dark and hot, how his teeth sank into his bottom lip.

"Look at her, Nick," he whispered hoarsely, trailing his fingertips across the top swells of her breasts. "Look how beautiful she is."

His request to Nick drove home the fact that she was with two men, sending lightning streaking through her veins, and her stomach did a flip-flop low down inside. Her pussy throbbed and she knew she was wet, probably wetter than she'd ever been in her life.

"Beautiful," Nick agreed, hands still caressing her thighs, getting closer and closer to that place she ached to be touched. She shamelessly parted her legs and a wicked smile curved his mouth. He shoved the skirt of her dress up to reveal her panties and both men's gazes dropped to between her legs. She closed her eyes against the scorching heat she saw in their eyes, and against the stabbing sensation in her pussy.

"Oh, Kaelin," Nick said. "Holy hell. These are the prettiest panties I've ever seen."

She couldn't even remember what she'd put on that morning, and lifted her head to look at the black lace triangle with pink velvet bows on her hips. Mmm, yes, these were a nice pair. Nick covered the front of her panties with his hand and pressed there. He slid his fingers lower, between her legs, cupped her pussy and she throbbed into his palm.

"So hot. I can feel how wet you are." Nick glanced at Tyler. "She's really wet."

Any other time, if they'd talked about her to each other in front of her like that, she'd have been annoyed, but at that moment it felt so hot, so *powerful*, to hear them, to know how much she was affecting them too. She felt beautiful. Desirable.

She studied their flushed cheeks and glittering eyes, let her gaze track down over their bodies gleaming with a faint sheen of perspiration. The temperature in the room had to be close to sauna-like, the way they were all burning up.

Like a dream, a fever dream, she let them slide her dress all the way down over her hips and off. Then Tyler refastened her arms to the headboard. "Don't worry, sweetheart. You're not getting free that easy."

She lay there before them in her bra and panties and they gazed down at her with hot eyes. Then Tyler sighed and slid his hands behind her back. "This has to come off."

Nick tugged her unfastened bra off, baring her to them. Her breasts felt full and lifted higher as she took a deep breath in, the tips hard and aching. She licked her lips and swallowed.

"Sweet Jesus," Nick muttered. He closed his eyes briefly. "So pretty, Kaelin."

"Oh yeah." Taylor sat back to admire her too.

She'd never experienced anything like this. Well duh. Of course she hadn't. But it was their slow and appreciative way of undressing her and touching her that she'd never experienced. Not that she had that much sexual experience. But most guys seemed to be in a big hurry to get her clothes off, grope her breasts, maybe give her nipples a little attention and then get inside her.

But not these two. They took their sweet time, drawing out every moment, every touch, every lingering look until need clawed inside her, consumed her, fiery heat torching her body, until she lay naked on the bed.

"Oh god," she whimpered, moving her legs restlessly. Nick slid a hand up the inside of her knee, sending more sparks sizzling over her skin. "Oh my god."

"Now," Tyler said, his mouth carnal as he looked down at her. "Now we get to taste you."

Her pussy spasmed in anticipation. She rolled her head on the pillow, relishing this moment of complete helplessness, of dark anticipation, of sweet surrender. She wanted to feel guilty about the pleasure, about the wickedness of it, but how could she, when all responsibility was taken away from her?

"Let us take you there," Tyler whispered. He met her eyes and something passed between them, something she thought was understanding. "You can't stop it now."

She gave a tiny nod, looked at Nick. He too seemed to know what she was feeling. "Give yourself over to it," he said. "And let us take over."

They'd already taken over. And yet, instead of powerless, she felt powerful. Instead of fearful, she felt strong. Instead of bound, she felt free, free from having to think, free from having to be responsible and good.

This was what she wanted. *They* were who she wanted. Tears stung her eyes and she blinked at their glimmering images.

"Yes," she said. "Do it. Take me there."

Chapter Seven

Tyler understood her.

He understood why she wanted to be tied up, he completely got it and he knew Nick sure as hell got it too. She wanted to be bad, but she wanted someone else to take control. The idea that sweet Kaelin Daume had these wicked urges nearly blew his mind, which was already sizzling and smoking with the heat and electricity jolting through his body. He probably only had a few functioning brain cells left.

Those few functioning brain cells were trying to tell him to stop. They were trying to tell him he was going to regret doing this to Kaelin, in essence taking her virginity. Okay, she likely wasn't a virgin, unless Cop Boy was actually gay, but Tyler was pretty sure she'd never done anything like this before and he was going to deflower her, so to speak. Debauch her. Corrupt her. Like he did everything else in his life. She was a glow of sweetness and goodness and unselfishness and he was going to take her and darken that glow.

Fuck.

But when he looked at her body, stretched out on the bed, arms bound above her head and her eyes watching him with heated arousal, those last few brain cells went up in smoke. She was gorgeous. She hid a sexy, sexy body beneath her modest clothing, but then he'd known from ten years ago what her body looked like in little cutoff shorts and bikinis. That summer...god, that summer she'd tortured him. It had been hot, hot and dry, and he swore every time he saw her she wore less and less.

He didn't know where to start with her, wanted to taste her, wanted to eat her up, basically inhale her. He could start at her mouth and work his way down. Or he could start with her toes and work his way up. He looked at Nick.

"Kiss her," Nick said.

Tyler's chest expanded and he shifted on the bed over her, while Nick moved down. Reaching for her face, he cupped her jaw and, stretching out beside her, he kissed her. Long, slow, wet. He slid his tongue into her mouth, rubbed his fingertips over her soft face, gently sucked her tongue, bit her lips so softly. Her soft little whimpers inflamed him and made him want to go faster, harder, but he leashed that urge and kept it slow and gentle. She was tied up. Couldn't go anywhere. There was no need to rush.

And she was right. This was one night. One night with Kaelin and then he'd have to get the hell out of town. Again.

Why did he keep screwing up his life?

He pushed that thought away to worry about later, right now was for Kaelin and making the most of this chance. He'd forgone this incredible gift ten years ago, tried to do the right thing, although somehow he'd screwed that up too, but this time he was taking it. He'd have to deal with the consequences, but he was taking it.

He licked her mouth, kissed her cheek, her jaw, breathed in that scent of fruit and flower, like green apple and honeysuckle, sweet and delicious. "You smell good," he murmured, nose pressed to her neck, filling himself with that warm and wonderful scent.

He shot a glance down her body and watched Nick lift one of her small feet and kiss it, his eyes closed, mouth open. So fucking hot.

Tyler opened his mouth on the side of Kaelin's neck and gently sucked, then kissed his way lower, over her collarbone and onto the soft flesh below. Her breast brushed his jaw and he forced himself to go slowly, to kiss between her breasts. She drew in a sharp breath and arched her back in a silent invitation.

Sweat built on his skin, heat rushed through his body. His dick rubbed against Kaelin's hip through his underwear and he wanted that barrier between them gone. He stripped off his boxer briefs and moved back beside her while Nick moved higher, kissing Kaelin's legs and parting them. The scent of her arousal rose to his nose and his cock twitched hard, blood pulsing through his veins in hot surges.

He lifted his head to gaze down at her, wanting the visual, wanting it all, the taste of her, the smell of her, and then, Christ yeah, the feel of her as he dragged his tongue over a nipple, all tight and hard. She gasped and he licked again, and then took her nipple into his mouth and sucked. It fit perfectly between his tongue and the roof of his mouth and she tasted like warm desire.

"Sweet baby," he mumbled against her flesh. "So damn sweet."

Her body writhed and again Tyler glanced at Nick, his hands now parting Kaelin's thighs, studying her, an absorbed expression on his face. He was about to send her rocketing up, and Tyler's body tightened even more. He cupped Kaelin's other breast and gently squeezed, resumed his suckling, then found her other nipple with his fingers and tugged.

She cried out and her pleasure sent a flash of fire through

him. Yeah, he wanted to please her, he wanted Nick to please her, he wanted the two of them to make this so good for her. Because if she was going to risk it all to be bad, it had better be good.

A nearly overwhelming sense of responsibility tore through him, unfamiliar and unsettling, but it did nothing to diminish his lust. He'd get his satisfaction too, he was sure of that, but first came Kaelin's.

Hopefully several times over.

He sucked and nibbled and licked both nipples until he lifted up to gaze down at them, reddened and stiff, shining in the lamp light. "Beautiful," he murmured. "So fucking beautiful."

Kaelin's eyes were closed, her head back, small chin lifted, her chest raised to him, and then he looked at Nick, who'd pushed her thighs wider, opened her with his thumbs and was licking her.

Again, beautiful. Nick's mouth on her, his tongue stroking her, and then his lips closing over her and sucking had Tyler reaching for his dick. He gave it several hard strokes, rubbed it against Kaelin's hip. He was wet and the slick head slid on her skin. He felt her tighten against him, watched her face as her mouth opened, eyes squeezed shut and she came, hard, lifting her hips into Nick's mouth, long, body-jolting pulses.

She didn't come in silence, letting her feelings out in her wordless cries of delight. Fuck, that was hot.

Nick slowly lifted his face from between her legs, his lips gleaming with her syrup and Tyler wanted to kiss him and lick her taste off his lips. He glanced at Kaelin, wondering how she'd take that. His chest tightened and he met Nick's eyes. How were they going to handle this?

Nick slid up the other side of her and instead kissed her,

and Tyler watched, his dick throbbing painfully.

"Oh my god," Kaelin moaned. "Oh my god."

"Was it good, honey?" Nick asked.

"Oh god, yes, so good." She still lay there, now limp, arms still stretched above her head. "You can untie me now."

"Oh no," Tyler said, stroking a hand over her stomach, rubbing in small circles. "Not yet."

Her eyes opened, dazed and foggy.

"We aren't nearly done, sweet baby," he said, fingers brushing the underside of her breasts. "Not nearly."

She blinked at him, her lips swollen, eyelids heavy.

"You said one night," he reminded her. "Just this one night. So it's going to be a long night, sweet baby."

Her eyes widened, then drooped again as both men touched her, ran their hands over her body, the curve of her shoulder, the inside of her slender arms, which made her shiver, then her waist and hip.

"What do you want, Kaelin?" Tyler asked, dipping his finger into her navel.

She just turned her head from side to side on the pillow and bit her bottom lip.

She couldn't ask for it. Somehow he had a feeling that all her life, what she'd wanted, what she'd needed, hadn't really mattered, that she'd always put aside her own wants and needs. And now she couldn't even ask for it.

He didn't know how far she'd thought this through, this being with two men, so they were going to have to explore and feel her out. Ha. Literally. He smiled as he moved his hand lower, brushed over the tiny puff of curls then slipped between her thighs.

Wet. So wet. He dragged his fingertips over soft, swollen

folds, cupped her pussy then slid his fingers deeper. He found the molten center of her, found her entrance and gently probed. Her moan encouraged him, and he played there more, spreading her slickness then pushing a finger deep inside her. Her hips moved on the bed.

Nick shifted and bent his head to Kaelin's breasts, taking his turn to taste their sweetness, again a visual that set off a firebomb of heat in Tyler's balls. Tyler divided his gaze between Kaelin's pretty breasts and Nick, and his own fingers in her pussy. And then, carefully, he slid his fingers lower yet, all slippery with her lubrication, to find her back entrance. She jerked and her eyes flew open.

He played there, just rubbing over the puckered opening, watching her expression, but she didn't stop him. Until he pressed his finger deeper.

Her mouth opened. "Tyler," she gasped.

He met her eyes. "Have you done that?" he asked quietly.

She rolled her head side to side.

"Do you want to do that?"

"I don't know."

He smiled. It wasn't a no, and he knew she wanted them to control things. But he really wanted to her to say it. Christ, his dick was so hard it hurt at the thought.

He dipped his head and took the nipple closest to him into his mouth, his face now so close to Nick's their hair touched, both of them suckling on her.

"God!" she cried. "Oh god, that's incredible."

"Mmm." He licked and then took the nipple between his teeth and bit, so gently, so carefully. Heat built higher and hotter inside him and he wasn't sure how long he was going to last.

His fingers returned to her clit, swollen and hard, and rubbed there. Her body began to vibrate against them. *Come for me, sweet baby.* He wanted to do that for her, to make her feel so good. Her soft sounds increased in tempo and volume and he kept his fingers moving until she cried out again, her pussy lifting against his hand as she came.

"Beautiful," he murmured with a last lick at her nipple.

Her breasts rose and fell as she panted for breath. "That was insane," she gasped. "I can't believe...I've never..."

Oh yeah, right, Cop Boy sucked in bed. She'd probably never had multiple orgasms. Tyler rolled his eyes as he fell to his back beside her. His cock pointed straight up and quivered and he had to stroke himself again, cup his throbbing balls.

"Kaelin." Her name emerged from his mouth hoarsely.

"Mmm."

"I want to fuck you."

She said nothing and he turned his head to look at her. She met his gaze and heat exploded between them. "I certainly hope so," she said, and he choked on a laugh.

"We're going to have to untie your arms," Tyler said regretfully. "They'll go numb if we leave them like that too long."

She searched his face with her gaze as he reached for the silk tie, understanding that yeah, he'd done this before. He released her arms and he and Nick each took one and gently lowered them, massaging her hands and the slight muscles in her arms.

"Okay?" Nick asked her. She nodded.

"I want you unbound when I fuck you," Tyler growled. It had to be that way. Yeah, he liked a little bondage, got off on control, but the one thing he'd never, ever do, to anyone, was fuck them while they were tied up. "Nick'll hold you." He met

Nick's eyes and understanding passed between them, as it always did, wordless and unspoken.

They both moved, Tyler down to the foot of the bed where he grabbed Kaelin's legs and dragged her toward him. But Nick slid off the bed.

"Hold on," he said, and disappeared into the bathroom, returning seconds later with a package that he opened with a rustle. Jesus. Thank Christ Nick still had a functioning brain, 'cause Tyler hadn't even thought of protection, which was damn stupid. With a look of gratitude, Tyler took the condom from him and quickly rolled it on while Kaelin watched and Nick climbed back on the bed, took hold of her hands and pinned them to the bed on each side of her head.

Her eyes flickered and she looked up at Nick. He smiled reassuringly at her.

"I don't need to be held down anymore," she said quietly. "And I want to touch you. Both of you."

Nick released her hands and bent to kiss her mouth while Tyler watched, throbbing with hot anticipation. The scent of feminine arousal filled his head, driving him insane with lust, and he gazed at her slender body, the lamplight gilding her curves, highlighting the dark curls above her pussy. Oh man. Something expanded inside him, thick and hot, almost scary. He bent his head to taste her, pressing his tongue to her sweet, hot center, and when her fingers slid into his hair and she murmured his name, he was lost. Consumed by fiery sensation, heat and light and urgent need. He licked her again, so gently, his tongue sliding over her liquid sweetness, finding her clit, so sensitive. He covered it with his mouth and sucked, but he didn't want her to come yet, so he lifted his mouth and moved over her. Her taste lingered in his mouth and their eyes met.

She spread her legs farther for him, her face luminous

below him, eyes big and dark, and he went onto his knees, widespread, and lifted her thighs. His cock nudged her entrance, scalding him with her wet heat and he groaned. "Kaelin. Oh god, Kaelin. Your pussy is so hot and wet. So sweet."

She focused on him, and that intense concentration on him alone went straight to his head. Nick's hands caressed her breasts, and when Tyler glanced at him, he saw Nick was focused too, his gaze intent on where Tyler and Kaelin were joined.

She made more soft little sex sounds as he eased into her, and she was so hot and tight he was afraid he wasn't going to get all the way inside her before he came. He gritted his teeth, withdrew and pressed in, again and again. She was fucking amazing, holding his cock in a tight grip, the friction of her slick inner walls like a drug, an intravenous drug shooting through his veins. The tingling at the base of his spine increased, the pressure built inside him, his balls boiling but he had to...had to make her...and then she touched herself, found her clit and rubbed, her eyes falling closed, head going back again, and as Nick pinched her nipples and Tyler gave one more hard thrust into her softness, she cried out again, a sound of pure ecstasy and delight and Tyler came too. Fire raced from his balls and out his cock and he too shouted and groaned his pleasure, the surge of sensation almost unbearable, his body jerking in wrenching pulses.

"Fuck," he gasped, collapsing over her. "Fuck me."

Her hands slid over his back, damp with sweat, holding him against her and he panted beside her as she too gasped for air. And then another hand, bigger, heavier, came to rest on his shoulder. Nick. Both of them touching him. For some reason that made him feel strangely emotional and his throat actually tightened up. Luckily no one could see his face and they all stayed like that for long moments while the room gradually stopped spinning and the heat scorching his body faded to a warm glow.

What had she done?

Kaelin knew she should feel something bad—guilt or regret or even shame.

But dammit, all she felt was a rapturous glow of pleasure, her body still pulsing around Tyler inside her.

It was hard to believe after all these years this had actually happened. Maybe it was just a dream, another of those erotic dreams she often had. But no. Tyler's body was hot and solid and heavy on hers, even though he took some of his weight on his elbows. And Nick sat beside them, stroking her damp hair off her forehead.

She would keep this memory for the rest of her life, and she passed the next few moments reliving every touch, every word, every sensation, storing them carefully away, wanting to be able to recall those details. The smell of Tyler's hair and skin, warm hints of exotic spice and cedar, the texture of his hair beneath her fingers, the satisfying fullness she felt with him inside her. The gentleness of Nick's touches, his fingers on her nipples, the sweetness of his tongue on her. The beauty of both their bodies, Nick so thickly muscled and brawny, Tyler's muscles leaner and more elegant.

"Am I squashing you?" Tyler murmured, lifting off her. Their skin clung damply, and as he withdrew from inside her she let out a soft sigh, disliking very much that feeling of separation.

"No, I'm fine."

Tyler disappeared into the bathroom, no doubt to get rid of the condom, and returned a moment later, walking across the room with long-legged athletic grace, naked and breathtakingly gorgeous. She sighed again.

Nick drew the covers up over all three of them, him on one side of her, Tyler on the other. What was supposed to happen now?

The two men slid their arms around her and pressed their heated bodies against her and she couldn't bring herself to move. She lay there between them, Nick petting her shoulder, Tyler's hand resting on her stomach. "I should go," she said, not moving a muscle.

"Stay," Nick murmured. "One night. Remember?"

"I'm hungry," Tyler said and amusement bubbled up inside her.

"There's a vending machine down the hall," Nick said.

"Huh." Tyler sounded interested but made no move, either. "Maybe in a few minutes."

They lay like that for a while, and Kaelin thought she might have drifted off to sleep, floating on a sensual cloud of pleasure, until the bed moved as Tyler hauled himself out of it. She watched him step into a pair of jeans he retrieved from his suitcase, zipping them but not buttoning them. They rode dangerously low on his hips and he turned his back to grab his wallet from the dress pants he'd had on earlier, giving her a view of the deep ridges of muscle on either side of his spine and the twin indentations at the base, the jeans so low she was afraid he might be soon revealing that incredible ass. "Back in a minute," he said, and left the room.

Kaelin turned her gaze to Nick, thinking he might be asleep, but he watched her solemnly. "Okay?" he murmured, lifting a hand to tuck a piece of hair behind her ear.

She blew out a breath. "Yes. I'm okay."

"You've wanted that for a long time."

She pressed her lips together, lowered her eyes and didn't answer.

"Or should I say, you've wanted *him* for a long time."

Her eyes flew up to meet his.

"It's okay, Kaelin. I understand. But I want you to know...I want you too."

Heat swept over her and her tummy did a flip. "Oh, Nick." She laid her hand on his cheek. While he didn't incite the same tornado of feelings inside her that Tyler did, she'd thought about him a lot too, that summer they'd hung out together, wondering what it would be like to kiss him, to touch him. She liked him so much, and there was no denying the physical attraction she still felt for him. So when he moved his face toward hers on the pillow, she met him halfway and kissed him back. Warm and gentle, his kiss had her skin tingling all over and her breasts aching again.

The door opened and shut. They dragged their mouths apart to look at Tyler, walking toward them in those sexy, low-slung jeans, the muscles of his abs outlined and disappearing in a V below the open waistband. Any woman who'd run into him in the hall had gotten a treat.

He lifted a brow at seeing them kissing but said nothing, tossing several bags onto the bed. From under one arm he pulled out two bottles of water.

Nick pushed up and reached for a bag. "Chips. Excellent."

"Plain and all-dressed. And Doritos."

The guys ripped open the bags and they sat there, Tyler cross-legged and bare-chested on the end of the bed, Nick still in his underwear and her naked with a sheet over her, devouring the junk food. God, Doritos had never tasted so good.

And then something struck her.

The hotel room had only one bed. The hotel room that Tyler and Nick were sharing.

Her fuzzy brain sharpened, thoughts coming together, and she paused with a chip halfway to her mouth. She tipped her head to one side, looked from Tyler to Nick and back again.

"What?" Tyler mumbled.

She swallowed. "I just noticed something."

"What?"

"This room only has one bed."

"Yeah." When Tyler's eyes met hers, she knew he knew what she was asking.

He looked at Nick. Nick looked at him. They both looked back at her.

Chapter Eight

In the space of seconds, about a million thoughts ran through Kaelin's head.

They were gay. They were a gay couple. Once in high school there'd been a crazy rumor about them, but she'd completely disregarded it because of Tyler's reputation with girls. They'd both dated lots of girls. Girls had been after both of them, all the time, but especially Tyler. She'd seen them together naked, but that didn't mean anything. But what other explanation could there be for sharing a bed? She was pretty sure two straight guys wouldn't share a bed. A hotel room maybe, but not a bed. Or would they? But after the things they'd just done with her, how could they...?

Confusion muddled her thinking as she watched them, waiting for them to say something.

"It's complicated," Tyler finally said, and took a swig of water from a bottle.

She stared at him. "Complicated?"

"As in, hard to explain."

She shook her head. If they were gay, how would she feel about that? Her chest tightened. "I guess it's none of my business," she finally managed to say.

"Fuck," Tyler muttered, swiping a hand over his face.

"I'd say after what just happened here, it kind of is your business," Nick said quietly.

"It doesn't matter," she said. Because really, it didn't. This was one crazy night of being bad. Their relationship with each other made no difference to her. But another thought intruded. Had she made them do something they hadn't wanted to? Oh, that was just a bit humiliating.

Tyler sighed and ran his hand through his hair. "Nick and I started fooling around in high school," he said, and she kept her jaw from dropping at the admission. Holy crap. "I don't even know if we can explain it. We both like girls too."

"I think we just wanted sex all the time," Nick added dryly.

"Actually, I think it might have had something to do with knowing how freakin' pissed off my parents would be if they found out." Tyler grimaced. "At least at first."

Oh lord. That was *so* Tyler, the bad-boy rebel. Wow. She kept listening.

"Neither of us has ever been with any other guy," Tyler told her. "It's just a...thing we have. With each other."

Kaelin caught a flicker of something on Nick's face. What was that? It almost looked like pain. She studied him as he shaped his expression back into neutral and met her eyes. He gave her a small smile and a shrug. "See? It's complicated."

"Uh-huh."

Her heartbeat kicked up a notch and her breath quickened.

"Does that disgust you?" Tyler asked, looking fully prepared for her to say yes.

She considered his question. No, she wasn't disgusted. Whatever she was feeling was nowhere even close to disgust. A bit confused maybe, a bit shocked. She looked back and forth between them. And realized she also felt intrigued.

Even...aroused.

"So," she said. "What happened tonight wasn't just you taking pity on me in my crazy desire to be bad. I mean, you were actually..." She lost her search for the right words.

Tyler's expression turned fierce. "Jesus, Kaelin. We were fucking *hot* for you. Couldn't you tell that?"

"Um, well, I thought you were, but..."

"Don't even doubt that, Kaelin." Nick leaned toward her. "I told you...I want you too."

She went soft and liquid inside at his words, and at the intense expression on Tyler's face when he'd said they'd been hot for her. "Um. Okay."

Tyler tossed aside an empty chip bag and screwed the cap back onto the bottle of water. He dropped it to the carpet beside the bed and moved purposefully toward her, and her heart sped up. Kneeling in front of her, he tipped up her chin and kissed her mouth. Hard.

After a few seconds of stunned inertia, the kiss changed as Kaelin opened for him and his mouth gentled on hers, his tongue licking inside her mouth. When he drew back they were both breathing hard. Nick moved off the bed briefly and then back in for another kiss. Kaelin lifted one hand and laid it on Tyler's chest, let the other rest on Nick's shoulder as the kiss deepened and grew hotter. Her pussy ached again and her skin started to tingle everywhere.

Nick reached for her and pulled her toward him, onto his lap, now naked, one hand on her hip, one in her hair and they kissed over and over in long, drugging kisses. Then her pulse skyrocketed when she felt Tyler's lips on her back. Heat rushed through her body and her head went light and fell back. Nick kissed her throat, small suckling kisses, moving down, resting on the pulse fluttering wildly at the base of her throat, then lower still. Her breasts ached to be touched, her nipples tingling points of sensation, while Tyler's lips on her back trailed streamers of pleasure over every nerve ending. Tyler's mouth moved lower too, until it came to rest at the base of her spine, his tongue licking her sensitive skin there. Her butt clenched, her entire body awash in a shimmer of erotic heat edged with a dark thrill and forbidden ecstasy.

When Nick took a nipple in her mouth, she couldn't stop the needy noise that escaped her throat, his lips tugging a streak of pleasure from nipple to pussy. Tyler's mouth at the base of her spine had her lifting up from Nick's lap in a wanton invitation which he accepted, kissing her butt cheeks. The thrill went beyond words, the wickedness of it tearing through her.

She whimpered.

Nick shifted them on the bed, which meant Tyler's mouth left her skin and she whimpered again, but Nick stretched out on the bed on his back with her lying on top of him. He took her hair in big fistfuls of it and held her head as he kissed her mouth again, her breasts cushioned against his hard chest, while Tyler resumed his naughty exploration of her backside. His nips with his teeth jolted her, his tongue soothed, and his fingers joined in the tour, tickling her where butt cheeks joined her thighs, where she was so sensitive she twitched and moaned at his touch.

"Babe, you are so hot," Tyler whispered from behind her.

Nick's cock throbbed hot and hard between them and the ache in her pussy made her move against him longingly, seeking what he had that could ease it. And then Tyler's fingers were there, slipping between her thighs, finding the liquid center of her.

"Hot," he murmured, stroking and dipping. "So hot, sweet baby."

"Mmm." She hummed her agreement as Nick's hands moved to her hips to lift her. When Tyler took hold of Nick's cock, she thought she might explode with heat and lust. At first she thought Tyler was jacking Nick, and that was hot, so hot, but then she realized he was rolling a condom onto Nick. They were both thoughtful and responsible that way, which caused a rush of emotion inside her. Then Tyler held Nick's cock while Nick lowered her onto it, and when his thickness filled her she moaned and buried her face into the side of Nick's neck.

"Oh, Kaelin." Nick's whisper held awe and heat. "You feel incredible. God…"

Tyler's wicked fingers lingered on her pussy as Nick filled her deeper and deeper, the sweetest friction inside her. And then Tyler trailed his wet fingers back and up, over the pucker of her rear entrance. She gasped against Nick's neck. His hands stroked up her back and tunneled into her hair again.

"S'okay, sweetheart." He turned his face and found her mouth with his.

Oh, this was so bad, so wanton, so incredibly hot and erotic. But she'd gone this far, she might as well turn herself over to it, let the pleasure consume her, let Tyler and Nick show her how bad she could be.

Nick rolled her to her back, still inside her, moved over her, in her, the friction of his flesh inside her a sweet swelling pleasure. And now Tyler was caressing Nick, kneeling behind him, his hands on his hips, his back, his ass. Tyler's face looking down at both of them was dark and tight, his eyes hot and heavy as his gaze moved from her face to Nick's body and back.

Nick made a noise deep in his throat and she knew Tyler had touched him, but she couldn't see what exactly he was doing. But Nick's body was going tight, his head went back, teeth gritted. "Oh Jesus," he gasped. "Tyler."

She thought she might pass out from the excitement of it, drowning, swept away, imagining Tyler's hands on Nick's balls, his thighs, his ass. Was he...oh she couldn't even think it, it was so erotic and wicked, and she longed to see what he was doing to Nick that was giving him so much pleasure.

Nick rubbed his rough face over her cheek, kissed her temple and moved over her, hands in her hair again, groaning his pleasure, thrusting, pushing up into her, finding that place, rubbing against her sensitive clit. It was there, right there, so close and she gasped and strained toward it until it burst over her in a shower of sparks and light. She cried out, pushed against him, pulsing around him and then he came too. She wrapped her arms around his big, sweat-dampened body and held him tight as shudders racked him, aware that Tyler was there, smiling, stroking and when she opened her eyes and met his, so searingly erotic, her whole body tightened in more hard pulses.

They lay there, the three of them, in the bed side by side, Kaelin in the middle. Tyler's heart still thudded and that was just from watching.

They'd had threesomes, shared girls, but never like this. They'd never let go with a girl like that. Maybe because it was Kaelin and they trusted her and were both probably still at least half in love with her. Shit. He rubbed his face and kept his hand over his eyes.

"Tyler."

"Yeah." His voice was scratchy.

"Why do you go to such lengths to annoy your parents?"

Jesus. He kept his eyes covered while he processed that. "I don't go to great lengths," he finally said. "It seems to happen no matter what I do."

She shifted toward him, half on top of him, and looked at him. She pushed his arm away and he let her, because keeping it there would have looked stupid. "That's not true," she said quietly. "You just told me that one of the reasons you and Nick...er, did what you did was to piss them off. That's pretty extreme, I'd say."

Tyler stared into her soft brown eyes. Hell. He felt as if she was looking right inside him and it made him want to cover his eyes again. "I only half meant that. They don't even know about us."

"Well, explain that half then. Why?"

"Oh hell, Kaelin. You can figure it out."

Her eyebrows slanted down and her pretty lips pursed. "No, I really can't."

He so did not want to talk about this.

"It's not that big a deal," he finally said. "My parents worshiped Avery, thought she could do no wrong. I was always a disappointment to them, because I wasn't like her. I didn't do that great in school. I was good at sports, but not good enough to satisfy them. They wanted both their kids to be getting awards, to be perfect. When I wasn't perfect, they didn't want anything to do with me. But when I got in trouble they were right there, all over that. After a while, I gave up trying to be as good as Avery. And I just tried to be....bad."

"Oh." Kaelin breathed out a soft sigh. "I see."

He closed his eyes against the sympathy on her face and leaned back against the headboard, the covers pulled over his hips. Kaelin propped herself up on her elbows to look at him. "It's not that complicated," he added. "Typical sibling rivalry."

"But you and Avery get along fine."

"We do now. When I was younger, I blamed her. Then one time she stuck up for me with Mom and Dad, and I knew it wasn't her fault. She was my big sister and she tried to look out for me, even though I was pretty much bent on self-destruction."

Kaelin nodded thoughtfully. She glanced at Nick, who'd turned onto his side and rested his head on one hand while he listened. "I guess I get it," she said.

"I was the loser younger brother," Tyler added, hating the bitterness that edged his voice. He'd thought he was long over this, but this trip home had resurfaced a whole lot of crap. "The one who was never good enough. The one who embarrassed my parents constantly."

"Not that that would take much," Kaelin said dryly, and he looked at her with surprise. Their gazes connected and she smiled. "Your parents are pretty obsessed with their image in the community."

"No shit," Tyler said. His smile went crooked.

"For what it's worth, I never thought you were a loser," she told him softly. "Even when you were Avery's little brother, I was totally intimidated by you."

He snorted. "Intimidated?"

"You were super cool," she said. "I envied you because you did whatever you wanted and didn't seem to care what people thought."

Tyler studied her pretty face, lifted a hand to push a long strand of hair back. "That kind of thoughtless disregard isn't something to admire."

"It was for me. You know how I am. I envied you for that. But when you made fun of me, I felt like a mouse, timid and afraid to do anything."

"I made fun of you a lot, didn't I." He said it as a statement, a heavy feeling settling in his gut.

"Yes."

"I'm sorry, Kaelin."

"I know why you did it," she said. "I guess I always sort of did."

"You hit the nail on the head last night when you told me I was covering up my own insecurities by mocking other people. That was exactly what I did. But..." He glanced at Nick, took in his attentive expression. "I don't do that as much anymore. Right?"

Nick smiled slowly. "Not quite as much, yeah."

"This trip home has been tough," Tyler added.

"You know, you could have a better relationship with your parents," Kaelin said, rubbing over his pecs. God that felt good. "If you tried. Maybe if you talked to them."

He shook his head. There was more to that than she knew, more than he had any intention of telling her. "Not gonna happen. They don't want that either."

"I think they do," she said slowly. "Your mom talks about you all the time, Tyler. She bragged about you to me, about your degree, the great job you got in Chicago, now you opening your own business."

"Because I've finally done something they can brag about," he said bitterly. "They still don't feel any differently about me."

"I don't think that's true."

"You heard my mom last night," Tyler said. "She immediately jumped to the conclusion that I'd done something to piss you off, when you slapped me. And guess what? She was right."

Kaelin pressed her lips together and said nothing. What could she say? It was true.

"I only came back for Avery," he said. "Because she's getting married and she wanted me here. I just want to get this damn wedding over with and get the hell back to Chicago."

She nodded but her eyelids lowered and he wished he hadn't expressed that quite so forcefully. Although they all knew this was definitely a one-night thing. It wasn't as if she didn't know he was leaving on Sunday. She'd said that herself.

She looked at Nick, then back at Tyler. "So your parents don't know about you and Nick?"

Tyler's mouth twisted. "I don't think so, but I think they know something, or suspect it anyway. I don't remember exactly when it happened, but back in high school, all of a sudden they didn't want me hanging around with Nick anymore. Even though they'd always thought he was a good influence on me."

"I tried," Nick drawled.

Kaelin smiled.

"I think they knew something was going on and they wanted to put a stop to it before it got out and ruined their precious reputation."

She nibbled her bottom lip and nodded. "Hmm. Maybe."

"We knew there were rumors going around about us," Nick said.

"But we didn't give a shit," Tyler added. "In fact, at that point I kind of enjoyed the idea that my parents would freak out about it, like I said. I know it was immature. But Jesus, we were young and I was messed up."

"Oh, Tyler. You couldn't have been that messed up. Look at you now. You have a successful career and a relationship with a great guy."

"It's not a relationship." Tyler didn't look at Nick. "Just so you know. I mean, yeah, we live together and we fool around and stuff, but..."

"We still date women," Nick added. "Well, Tyler does more than I do. Someday he's going to meet the right woman and he'll get married and..." His voice trailed off but he smiled. "Right, Tyler?"

Tyler knew Nick's feelings for him were different than his feelings for Nick. He loved the guy, and yeah, there was sexual attraction, and Nick knew him better than anyone in the world and loved him despite that. But Tyler knew himself too, and knew if he was going to fall in love, the forever kind of love—and that was a big *if*—it was going to be with a woman. Nick accepted that, and though they'd never had any kind of deep discussion about it, Tyler kind of suspected Nick hoped that was never going to happen. It was one of those deeply awkward, uncomfortable topics they successfully avoided ever having to discuss, though it always lurked there below the surface.

"Right." He met Kaelin's eyes. "I know it sounds weird, but that's the way it is for us."

"I can't say I totally understand," she said, but she smiled. "But I don't think any kind of love can ever be bad. If you care about each other, that's all that matters. Thank you for telling me about that. I'm honored that you trust me enough. And thank you for sharing each other with me tonight."

Tyler's heart tightened at her words. She was thanking him. Jesus god, what had he done to deserve thanks? He reached for her and hauled her onto his lap, wrapped his arms around her and kissed her, long and desperate and wild. Her hands slid into his hair and she kissed him back. When they finally moved apart, panting, they both looked at Nick.

"Come here," Kaelin whispered. She extended a hand to

Nick, and Tyler did the same, glad that she had said that, because he felt the same way. He had pretty strong feelings for Kaelin, always had, but he didn't want Nick to feel excluded. Because even though Nick loved him, Tyler knew Nick cared about Kaelin too.

Nick moved on the bed, closer, until he was sitting right beside them, and he laid a hand on Kaelin's back. Their three faces were so close together. Tyler wanted to kiss Nick, to reassure him, of what he wasn't sure. This was a crazy one-night thing and didn't change anything for them. But Tyler looked at Kaelin, unsure what she'd think about that.

Understanding and warmth filled her eyes when he met them, and she leaned to kiss Nick herself. And then she drew back and said, "Go ahead. Kiss him."

Tyler held her gaze for a long moment then turned his face toward Nick, his strong-jawed face, his clear and steady silvery gaze. And Nick moved too, and their mouths met in a hot, clinging kiss.

Chapter Nine

Kaelin watched the two men kiss, heat sliding over her, through her. Her own mouth parted almost hungrily as their mouths met. Softness expanded in her chest, stealing her breath. She watched Tyler's hand come up to Nick's face, their eyes closed, open mouths fused. Oh. Oh wow.

After a long, deep kiss, they slowly drew apart and both men looked at her. She gave them a shaky smile, unprepared for how she felt about watching them. Emotional. Aroused.

She knew she liked to watch, though she'd kept that kink buried deep inside her along with her desire to be tied up. There'd always been a forbidden thrill about watching, along with a measure of guilt too, going way back to the time when she was a teenager and had been in the park, sitting on a bench reading a book and had seen a couple, strangers, stretched out on a blanket not far away, making out. She'd watched them over the top of her book, guilty but turned-on.

And that night she'd walked in on Tyler and Nick and that girl, she'd stood behind the door and watched way too long, hurt and shocked, but fascinated, with prurient interest.

But she'd never dreamed about watching this. Tyler and Nick. Two men. It surprised her, but on another level, it felt so completely right. The way they looked at each other, the emotions she sensed between them, the ease with which they touched each other, so comfortable and confident, it made it beautiful to watch. Absolutely, heart-meltingly beautiful.

"Let's lie down," Tyler said, shifting her off his lap. "Need a rest." They arranged themselves under the covers, Kaelin in the middle on her back, the guys on their stomachs, each with an arm flung across her. The heat from their big bodies warmed her, their arms pleasantly heavy on her. She kept thinking about that kiss, awareness now acute that the two men on either side of her probably wanted to touch each other as much as they wanted to touch her. And she wanted that too.

If she was going to have this one wicked night, she might as well have it all.

"Have you ever thought about moving?" Tyler asked.

Huh? She turned her head on the pillow to look at him. "What do you mean?"

"Moving. Away from Mapleglen."

"Um. Well. Not seriously."

"But you've thought of it?"

Why was he asking her this?

"Avery wants me to move to Los Angeles." She closed her eyes and pressed her face against Tyler's shoulder, found Nick's hip with one hand. "But I can't move away from here."

"Why not?"

Just like his sister, he didn't accept her answer. Why not? Why couldn't they understand that this was her life? She'd lived here since she was born and didn't know anything else. "Because I have my job here. A life here." Not much of a life lately, but still... "I have my house. My dog."

"Why'd you move back here? After college?" Tyler asked.

"I had to." She turned her head to look at him. "My mom died just after I finished college. My dad...well, you know about him."

"Not very much, actually."

She'd assumed everyone knew about her dad and what had happened to him. "He was hurt in an accident at work," she told them. "When I was fourteen. He had a broken arm and leg and a head injury. His arm healed, but not his brain." She sighed, remembering how physically he'd looked the same, big and strong, but he'd never been the same person again. Instead he'd been like a child, with poor impulse control, no short-term memory and no inhibitions. Her dad had been taken away from her in that accident and had never come back. "The first few years after his accident were hard," she continued. "It was like he was a different person. We had some help, but mom started working night shifts at the hospital so she could be home during the day. My dad didn't have much insight into what had happened to him and lived happily on in his own world. But he couldn't be left alone for any length of time because he'd do things like leave the stove on or cut his finger off with a knife, so we had to try to be there as much as we could for him."

Part of the reason her teenage social life had been so dismal. Why so many nights, including Saturday nights, had been spent at home studying. Although it had been important to her to get good marks, she'd also felt an obligation to help out and look after her dad.

"It was really hard on my mom, looking after him all by herself while I was away at college, but she was managing. But then she got breast cancer. I'd been hoping to go to law school, but that was okay." It really wasn't. She'd wanted to practice law pretty much her whole life, had done well in college, and had aced her LSAT, but when she'd had to come home to Mapleglen, she'd pushed away the disappointment to do what had to be done.

Tyler stroked her hair.

"My mom didn't discover the cancer until it was too far advanced to do anything. I don't think she looked after herself very well. After she died, I had to stay home to look after my dad, but a few years later he had a stroke. Probably a consequence of the brain injury." She closed her eyes remembering the loss of her parents so close together. It had been a few years, so it wasn't as painful as it once was.

"I'm sorry." Tyler said the words, and Nick added, "Me too, Kaelin."

"It's okay."

"What about going back to school? Ever think of that?"

All the time. "Sometimes, yeah. But I like my job. And you know what they say—a bird in the hand is worth two in the bush. I figured I was better to hang on to what I had here—a job, a home, friends—than to give it up and go after something unknown." Something scary.

The men were silent.

"I know that's not how you live your lives," she whispered. "But it's how I live mine."

Tyler rolled to face her and his blue eyes studied her. "As long as you're happy," he said. "That's what counts. Are you happy here, Kaelin?"

She stared back at him, a tightness in her chest, an ache deep inside.

"Of course I am," she lied.

He nodded, looking as if he didn't believe her, but pulled her up against him, Nick warm and big on her other side.

"What about you two?" she asked. "You're happy in Chicago?"

"Yeah. I love it there," Tyler said. "So much energy, so

117

much happening."

"And your business is going well."

This time Nick answered. "Pretty good."

She turned back to him. "That didn't sound enthusiastic."

Nick grinned. "We've only been in business a year. It takes a few years to get going, but we're doing okay. We actually made money the first year, which is unusual."

"He's the numbers guy," Tyler said. "I'm the creative. We're in the middle of trying to sign a big new client, but we're having a...hmm...difference of opinion on it."

"Who's the client? What's the problem?"

"The client is Healthy Solutions."

"Wow. Big company."

"Oh yeah," Tyler said. "Huge. This would really establish us in the advertising business in Chicago."

"In the whole country," Nick said, but his mouth twisted.

"So what's the problem?" Kaelin looked back and forth between them, rolling her head on the pillow.

Tyler propped his head up on an elbow. "What's the problem, Nick?"

Nick also rose, and the two men looked at each other across her. Oh-oh. She hadn't meant to start a battle here. There was clearly some tension between them over this.

"The stuff they sell is useless crap," Nick said.

"Oh." Well that was blunt.

"Their image is all natural and healthy and herbal products," Nick continued with heat in his voice. "But that stuff doesn't do shit. They're taking advantage of people, selling dreams."

"That's what advertising is," Tyler said. "It's not up to us to judge the products."

"I think it is."

"We can't do that in every case! You think we should never advertise condoms because of moral reasons? Come on."

"We're not talking about condoms, which is a whole other tricky issue. We're talking about creams that will increase a woman's bust by two cup sizes."

Kaelin perked up. "There's a cream that will do that?"

They both gave her a look.

"I'm kidding," she said, relaxing again. "Healthy Solutions sells that?"

"Yeah. Along with herbal pills for erectile dysfunction and whole bunch of different cures for cancer."

"Oooh." Yeah, that was low. "But don't they sell vitamins too? They're in all the drugstores."

"Yeah, and their vitamins are legit. Which is probably why the company has a good reputation."

"This contract could make us financially secure," Tyler said.

"Make us or break us," Nick said. "We need to have some ethics."

"You're saying I have no ethics?" They locked glares.

"I see the problem," she said.

"What's your advice, Kaelin?" Tyler shifted his gaze to her, and it softened, a teasing light in his eyes.

"I don't know anything about advertising," she said, eyes flicking back and forth between them. "Other than you do make people buy things they don't need."

"Oh!" Tyler's eyes widened. "You're a critic of the advertising business too!"

She smiled. "No. But we live in a society that values consumption. Build more, manufacture more, sell more. Go into debt more buying things you don't need."

Nick laughed. "You are so right, honey. That's what I'm talking about."

"It's the American way," Tyler said.

She laughed. "Nick's right. You have to have some ethics."

Tyler sighed. "You're so sweet, Kaelin."

Sweet. Even after all that, they still thought she was sweet. Ah well. She snuggled down in between them again. She may have drifted off to sleep for a little while, and maybe Tyler and Nick did too, she wasn't sure. When their hands started moving on her body in slow caresses, she floated on an erotic cloud of sensation. Hands on her shoulders, sliding between her breasts, over her arms. Her body stirred, her legs shifted on the smooth sheets. Fingers brushing over the curls at the juncture of her thighs, tracing around her navel, cupping her breast. She sighed.

A mouth opened on her shoulder in a hot kiss. A hand lifted her hand and she dragged her eyes open to watch Nick kiss her fingers. His own eyes heavy-lidded, he watched her face. She smiled.

Tyler moved beside her and she turned to him as he bent his head to one breast, taking her sensitive nipple between his lips and sucking. Heat spiraled from nipple to womb and she gasped. Then Nick sucked her other nipple, as they had before, both at the same time. Two mouths on her tender nipples. The overload of sensation made her shudder and her pussy clench as heat rippled through her body. But this time she looked at their two heads, so close together, Tyler's tousled gold hair next to Nick's short dark bristle. This time she set her hands on their heads, holding them there as they suckled her, and when they lifted their heads she gently pushed them together.

Tyler shot her a look, but he kissed Nick again, right there in front of her, only inches away, another long deep kiss and his tongue licked over Nick's bottom lip. Kaelin moaned.

"Yes," she whispered. "That's what I want."

"Mmm?" Tyler's mouth slid off Nick's. He lifted an eyebrow. "You want to watch us, sweet baby?"

She licked her lips and gave a short nod. "You can...touch each other. You know." She searched for words. "Do whatever you want. With each other."

Heat flashed into her face at her stumbling attempt to tell them what she wanted.

They both knelt beside her. "But this is all about you tonight," Nick murmured, kissing her collarbone.

"It doesn't have to be," she protested, lifting her head from the pillow. Tyler pushed her back down, gently, with a smile.

"I know what you mean," he said. "Thank you, Kaelin."

He was thanking her? For wanting to watch them together? Her mind was a little fuzzy with lust, but, okay, whatever.

"Are you sore?" he asked, slipping his fingers between her thighs.

"Er...maybe a little." She blinked up at them.

They did another of those wordless communications that she now knew went so deep. And then Nick reached for Tyler's cock, already standing at attention. Kaelin swallowed as his big hand wrapped around the base. Tyler set a hand on Nick's shoulder and his eyes closed and his head fell back as Nick stroked him above Kaelin's body. She scrambled to sit up and lean against the headboard, pulling the sheet with her. It only reached to her waist and she looked down at herself. Guess it didn't really matter whether she was covered at that point.

She turned her attention back to the tableau in front of her. Nick and Tyler moved closer together and kissed again, still on their knees, Nick still pulling Tyler's cock. Nick's own cock bobbed and, unable to resist, Kaelin extended her hand to stroke him. He was long and thick, smoother than Tyler's heavily veined cock, with a pronounced ridge around the crown, both of them so, so beautiful. Her mouth watered at the sight and her lips parted. Nick broke the kiss to look down at her touching him and smiled at her.

"I want to suck you," she whispered.

"Oh yeah," he groaned. Nick moved on his knees closer to her, straddled her body, and she adjusted her position on the bed to be able to take him into her mouth. He groaned again as she sucked on just the head then licked him, holding his throbbing heat in her hand. She loved doing this, loved the feel of him pulsing and alive in her hand, in her mouth, loved the texture of his skin on her tongue, the salty taste of precome leaking from the tip.

"Perfect," Tyler said from above Nick's shoulder. He'd moved up behind Nick and watched. Kaelin looked up at both of them, her mouth full. She hummed her agreement and Nick's body jolted.

Tyler's hands slid down over Nick's chest, rubbed over his nipples, and Nick twitched again in her mouth. She tightened her mouth on his shaft, trying to keep the rhythm while she watched Tyler caress Nick's chest, rub his face against Nick's jaw, and kiss his shoulder. It was like a dream, watching that, seeing Tyler, always so tough and mocking and cynical, now tender and gentle. Once again, emotion rose in her and she closed her eyes as she sucked on Nick, so delicious, filling her mouth so perfectly.

"Gonna fuck you," Tyler muttered, one hand going to Nick's

forehead and pulling his head back. "While Kaelin sucks you." A long groan tore from Nick's throat as Tyler released him then pushed him forward. Nick braced his hands on the headboard above Kaelin's head and bent forward as much as he could. She had to adjust a little, squirmed a little lower, shoved pillows behind her. Heat flowed through her veins, anticipation sizzling through her at what was about to happen. Tyler crowded up behind Nick, on his knees, slid an arm around his waist. Nick's eyes were closed. Kaelin paused in what she was doing to catch her breath, to wait for it...she couldn't see but knew Tyler had his cock in his hand and was pressing against Nick's ass. She kept stroking Nick, though with her hand.

"Yeah," Nick said. Perspiration shone on his chest and shoulders, every big muscle in his arms hard and defined as he tensed up, gritted his teeth. "Oh yeah."

She found his balls with her other hand, cupped them gently, rolled them against her palm, and then curiously, daringly, she slid her fingers farther back over hot damp skin stretched taut until she bumped against Tyler's cock buried in Nick's ass. And then she reached farther still and stroked over Tyler's testicles, tight in their sac.

"Kaelin." Tyler bent over Nick's back, now both arms around him, rubbing his chest and abs. "Christ, Kaelin."

She smiled, licked her lips and resumed sucking hungrily on Nick, fingers playing delicately over male flesh, fingernails scraping. Tyler's rhythm picked up pace, pushing Nick's cock deeper and deeper into her throat, too deep, and she had to pull off with a gasp.

"Sorry," he grunted. "Sorry, sweet baby."

"Fuck me, Tyler," Nick groaned. "Harder. Oh god, both of you like that...unbelievable."

This time Kaelin lifted Nick's cock and used her tongue to

explore his balls, and Tyler's too, drawing curses from the two men as Tyler fucked Nick, faster and harder.

"Gonna come," Nick gasped. "Kaelin..."

She'd wanted him to come in her mouth, but his orgasm exploded so fast, he came on her shoulder instead. She shifted back, held his cock, stroked it as he came, more spurts landing now on her breasts. Oh lord, that was hot, so damn hot, she was going to burst into flames.

Tyler rose up straighter, pulling Nick with him, one hand on his chest, the other on his forehead, and Nick twisted to kiss him as they went still, low sounds of pleasure rumbling in Tyler's throat as he came too. She cupped Tyler's balls and felt them pulse in her hand and he tore his mouth away from Nick's to give a wordless shout.

"Fuck," Nick gasped. "Holy fuck."

Kaelin stroked his hips, the strong square bones, the soft skin beside his groin, his hair-roughened thighs, then slipped her hands around him to caress Tyler's ass, the muscles there rock hard. She pressed her cheek to Nick's thigh and hugged them both.

Oh lord. Oh lord. Eyes closed, breathing in the scent of semen and sweaty male skin, Kaelin's mind tumbled. This was more than she'd ever fantasized about, hotter and more wicked than her imaginings, but on top of that it was deeply, emotionally moving. She couldn't analyze why, not just then, her head spinning, her brain short-circuiting. Maybe sometime she'd think about it. Or maybe not. Maybe it was better not to.

She took a deep breath and released them from her embrace, fell back onto the mattress. "Oh my god," she said.

She looked up at them, Tyler's arms sleek with muscles and golden hair still around Nick's torso, his big muscular body. Nick's head was back on Tyler's shoulder, their eyes were closed, and then they opened their eyes and looked down at her. She gazed helplessly back at them, struck speechless by the beauty of their bodies and their feelings for each other.

"Kaelin." Tyler and Nick separated and fell to the bed on either side of her. "That was unbelievable."

She gave them a shaky smile and a nod. They'd done this before, though, probably lots of times, with women hotter and more sexually experienced than she. And she had to wonder, why did they even need a woman? They obviously loved being together. For some reason, that thought made her eyes sting and her throat go tight.

But why? It wasn't as if she was ever going to see them again after this weekend. They never came back to Mapleglen and Tyler apparently had no intention of trying to patch things up with his parents. Probably the next time she'd see him would be at a funeral, in about twenty or thirty years.

"Kaelin." Tyler repeated her name again, his arm across her breasts, his hand on her cheek. "We've never done anything like that before."

She turned to him wide-eyed. "What?"

He met her gaze steadily. "We've had threesomes before," he said, his voice low and husky. "But no girl has ever done that for us...touched us both...let us do that."

She opened her mouth, but nothing came out. She blinked. Then finally she said, "Really?"

Nick moved on her other side, stroking her shoulder and arm. "Really."

"Oh."

Wow. Once again, she wasn't sure what it all meant. And then, as they lay there quietly, the overload of sensation and emotion took over and she fell asleep.

Tyler stretched in bed, a warm body next to him. A soft, warm body. Nice. He reached for it, pulled her closer. Mmm. Kaelin. Her butt fit perfectly in his groin, and his hand found a soft breast, tipped with a velvety nipple. Really nice. He nuzzled into her hair, smelling sweetly of honeysuckle and apples, and prepared to drift back to sleep in that position.

She wriggled her ass enticingly and his morning erection stirred. He smiled against her hair. God, could they really go another round? She was pretty amazing.

"Oh my god!" Her voice split the silence in the dark hotel room and she bolted out of his arms. Adrenaline flashed through his veins and he sat up.

"What? What's wrong?"

Nick sat up too on the other side of the bed, rubbing his eyes and squinting.

"It's almost noon!" Kaelin stood beside the bed, staring at the hotel alarm clock. Yep, those red numbers spelled out 11:52.

Oh Jesus. The wedding.

Tyler scrubbed a hand over his face. "Don't panic," he said. "The wedding's not until four."

"I know, but I have things to do! I have to pick up flowers, decorate the banquet room, the church, put out the favors. I have to get ready...omigod, omigod, omigod."

She frantically searched the room for her clothes, finding her dress, her bra. She struggled into the little black dress, now wrinkled as hell, then picked up her bra and stared at it. She stuffed it into her purse.

"I can't find my underwear," she muttered, turning in a

circle. Twice. Tyler hauled himself out of bed and caught her as she turned her back to him, then drew her zipper up, resisting the urge to drag his tongue up her bare back. "Oh, never mind. Omigod."

Bright sunlight glared around the edges of the heavy drapes over the hotel window. Shit. They did a good job of blocking the light and they'd all slept like they'd died, right through the morning. "What do you need us to do?" he asked, handing Kaelin her sandals. She grabbed them.

"Nothing. I don't know. Omigod." She tried to get the strappy high-heeled sandals on, stumbling and almost falling. Tyler let her use him to balance on while she slipped them on.

"Yes there is. We'll do whatever." He glanced at Nick who nodded and threw back the covers. "Where are you going first?"

"First?" She gazed blankly at him. "First I'm going home. I can't go around like this! In the same clothes I wore last night! What will people think?" She closed her eyes. Her hair hung in long tangles down her back and her mascara was smudged under her eyes in a way Tyler thought was damn sexy, but yeah, she probably didn't want to be running around town like that.

"I'll come with you," he said.

"No! Jesus. Are you crazy?"

"No one knows what happened last night," he tried to soothe. He attempted to smooth her hair. She swatted his hand away. "I'll drive you home. Nick'll meet us at the flower shop. We'll help you decorate. Don't worry, it'll all get done."

She sucked in a long shaky breath, staring at him with those big brown eyes, so sweet and sexy.

A buzzing sounded in her purse. She blinked, then groped in the big leather bag and pulled out her cell phone. Still looking dazed and disoriented she peered at her phone. "It's

Maddie," she whispered. "Omigod, she's staying here in the hotel."

She looked at Tyler, panic filling her eyes.

"She doesn't know you're here," he said quietly. "But don't answer it, if you're not ready."

She nodded, pressed a button that silenced the buzz, then covered her eyes with one hand. "Okay, I have to go."

"Just let me get dressed."

"No! I said it's okay, I've got my car. Gotta go. See you guys later."

And she flew out the door.

Tyler turned and scowled at Nick. "Thanks for the help, buddy."

"Christ, I'm still asleep, man." Nick shook his head. "Sorry, but you know I'm not awake until my third cup of coffee."

Coffee. That sounded good.

"We must have had about two hours sleep last night."

Tyler grinned. "I'm not complaining. Holy hell. What was that?"

Nick's eyebrows drew together above his nose. "I don't know. But I hope she's okay."

"Kaelin? Why? Because she left in such a hurry?"

"No. Because she stayed."

Chapter Ten

Kaelin's heart raced as she waited for the elevator, waiting for someone she knew to step out of a room, like Scott or Hardeep or Maddie. No, their rooms weren't on this floor. But still. Someone else she knew could be staying there. She looked at her watch, nibbled her lip, and when the elevator arrived, thankfully empty, she bolted into it and stabbed the button for the lobby. She slumped against the wall. Dear god, what had she done?

Well, she had no time for regrets or analysis or even some pleasurable memories, she had a gazillion things to do. She rushed out of the elevator, remembered there was a back door so she could avoid the lobby and headed that way. Her car was out front, but oh well, she'd just jog around the hotel to it.

In high-heeled sandals and a black silk cocktail dress. The late June day was hot already, the sky a perfect clear blue, the sun directly overhead. Finally she arrived at her car, sweaty and breathless. With no underwear, beard burn on her chin and who knew where else, mascara under her eyes and her hair in knots. Jesus.

She slammed the car into gear and peeled out of the parking lot. She had to get home, take a shower. She probably smelled of sex and Tyler's cedar and spice aftershave. Her tummy did a little flip and she groaned out loud, hands tight on the wheel. She must have lost her mind last night.

Not now, not now. She had to focus. She was supposed to pick up the flowers before noon then take the bouquets to the Wirth home. The big arrangements for the church were being delivered as well as the centerpieces for the tables, but she was supposed to meet the delivery guy at each place to give instructions on where to put everything. All the decorations and favors were at her place.

She chewed the inside of her lip as she drove on autopilot, so at first she didn't even notice the flashing lights behind her. When the police car whooped its siren at her, she jumped. Her eyes flicked to the rear-view mirror then forward again. She frowned. He couldn't be pulling her over. Could he? Maybe he just wanted to pass her. But no. When she pulled up at the curb, the police car pulled in behind her.

She dropped her head to the steering wheel. No. No, no, no.

When she turned to open her window, Brent stood there. Oh, thank god. He wouldn't give her a speeding ticket.

The window lowered at her touch on the button.

"I thought that was you," he said.

"Brent! What are you doing? You scared the crap out of me."

He frowned at her. "You were going kind of fast, Kaelin." He studied her hair, her face, her braless breasts beneath her wrinkled silk dress. "Are you okay? You look..." His voice trailed off.

Heat scorched her cheeks and washed its way down under that silk dress. "Yes, I'm fine, but I'm late...the wedding... Are you giving me a ticket?"

"I should."

She lost patience. "Well, then do it, and do it quick. I'm in a hurry."

His frown intensified. "Kaelin."

She wanted to scream.

"Where are you going?" he asked.

"Home!"

Then his eyes narrowed even more as he studied her clothing and she knew, she just knew, he recognized that she was wearing the same clothes she'd had on at the police station last night.

"Where were you?" he asked.

She gritted her teeth. "That isn't really your business. Seriously, Brent, I need to go. Can you mail me the ticket or something?"

He stared at her, and she saw emotions flicker over his face—disappointment, hurt, anger. *Shit.*

"No," he said. "I can't. License and registration, please."

"Forget Me Not Flowers," Avery said. "On Main Street downtown."

"I know it. Okay, thanks." Tyler snapped his phone shut as he strode through the lobby of the hotel with Nick. "Okay, now we know where she's going. We'll meet up with her there."

"Why isn't she answering her cell phone?" Nick muttered.

"I don't know. Maybe she's in the shower or something."

"Maybe we should go to her place."

They got into Tyler's Jeep. Should they? It had been half an hour since she'd rushed out. He and Nick had showered and dressed in record time, grabbed coffees to go from the hotel restaurant and were now trying to track down Kaelin so they could help her get done what needed to be. If they drove there, they'd likely miss her and then they might miss her at the florist. Shit. This was stupid. Why couldn't she just have waited a few minutes?

He parked on Main Street, a block away from the flower shop, and they loped up the street. He'd thought he didn't miss Mapleglen, but the downtown was kind of pretty with its brick sidewalks, vintage-style streetlights and baskets of bright hanging flowers everywhere. They shoved into the flower shop, which smelled all fresh and green and flowery.

"Hi." Tyler greeted the young girl behind the counter with a grin. "We're here to help pick up the flowers for the Wirth-Richards wedding."

She smiled at him, straightened her shoulders and flicked back her long blonde hair. "Oh yes. They're all ready."

"So Kaelin Daume hasn't been in yet?"

"No." The young girl blinked. She checked the order. "She was supposed to pick them up before noon, actually."

Tyler shot a glance at Nick. Should they take them and go? Wait for her? Then he got a thought. What if something had happened to her?

That was crazy. This was Mapleglen and she'd just left the hotel less than an hour ago, fine, although flustered. But maybe she shouldn't have been driving when she was all distracted. Again, shit. He tapped his fingers on the glass counter.

The shop phone rang and the girl smiled as she held up a finger and answered it. "Oh yes!" she exclaimed. "Good timing. Your, um....someone is here to pick up the flowers." She moved the phone away from her mouth. "Your name?" she asked Tyler.

"Tyler Wirth."

"Oh. Of course." She spoke into the phone again. "Mr.

Wirth is here to pick them up. Shall I send them with him?" She listened, nodded, said, "Of course." And handed the phone to Tyler. He tried to not to rip it out of her hand.

"Kaelin? Where are you?"

Her voice sounded funny. "I'm on my way home. Again."

"What happened?"

"You won't believe it."

Now she sounded pissed. What was going on?

"Are you okay?"

"I'm fine. But now I'm running even later."

"We're getting the flowers," he said, keeping his voice calm. "What else do we need to do?"

"They need to be dropped off at your mom and dad's place. They should be put in the fridge."

"No problem. What else?"

She sighed. "That's enough. I'll just go straight to the church."

"We'll meet you there."

"No, you don't—"

"Bye, Kaelin." He handed the phone back to the girl before Kaelin could argue with him. He gave her another of his most charming smiles. "Thanks. We'll take the flowers."

They put them in the back of the Jeep, drove back to his parents' place, encountering Avery dressed in a butt-ugly terry cloth robe with a towel turban on her head. "Nice," he said. "Is that your dress?"

"Smart-ass. Why are you bringing these and not Kaelin?"

"She's running late," he said, making room in the refrigerator.

"How do you know?"

"Never mind."

He stood and closed the door, the bouquets safely resting in coolness. He brushed his hands together.

"Tyler, what are you doing?" His mother appeared in the door, also in her bathrobe, her forehead furrowed.

"We're going to help her decorate now," he said, starting for the door.

Avery followed them to the door. "Maddie's supposed to help."

"Um. Yeah." Had Kaelin finally answered her phone? His gut clenched with worry, something very unusual for him. "She'll find us."

"Kaelin's supposed to be here by two," she called to them from the front door as they hoofed it down the sidewalk.

Tyler snorted and jumped into his Jeep. Not damn likely. "She might be a few minutes late," he called to her and his mom, both standing there gaping at them, and he and Nick pulled out, leaving them staring after them.

"Nice," Nick said. "Nobody's wondering anything."

"Fuck off."

Nick just shook his head, smiling.

Tyler returned to the church where they'd just had the rehearsal the night before. Christ, that seemed liked days ago. They pulled up out front at the same time as Kaelin. She jumped out of her Mazda, wearing jeans and a snug little T-shirt and flip-flops. Not the ladylike attire he'd seen her in the last couple of days. Huh.

Her hair was wet, she had no makeup on and her cheeks were red. She didn't seem to notice them, instead raced up the front steps to greet the delivery guy standing there, leaning against the doors looking annoyed.

"Sorry I'm late!" she said to him. "You can bring everything in now."

"Kaelin."

She whirled to face them. "Oh. Hi, guys. Did you get the bouquets?"

"You bet. Safe and sound and waiting for you. What do we need to do here?"

They helped carry in the massive arrangements of flowers. Tyler had no clue what they all were, big fluffy pink ones, small fuchsia ones, waxy white ones, lots of greenery. They set them up at the front of the sanctuary on either side of the altar. Then they helped her decorate the oak pews with bows and small sprays of flowers.

"So what happened to you?" Tyler asked.

She sighed. "I got a speeding ticket."

His head snapped up. "You're shitting me."

"I wish I was." He watched her mouth press together. "It was Brent."

Tyler paused in the act of attaching a satin bow. "And he gave you a fucking ticket?"

"Watch your language. We're in church."

Nick choked on a laugh. "Seriously, Kaelin, he gave you a ticket?"

"Yes." She scowled at the flowers in her hand. "I think he sort of figured out what happened last night. I was still wearing the same clothes and..." She looked around the church as if to make sure the minister wasn't within earshot.

"Sweetheart, nobody could even *imagine* what happened last night," Tyler said. "Which reminds me. Your panties are sitting on the desk in our room." She glared at him and he firmed his lips to keep from laughing. "Sorry."

"Whatever. He wasn't impressed." She took a long breath in, then out, stood back to survey their work then nodded. "Okay, we're done here. Now back to the hotel." She glanced at her watch.

They found Maddie waiting in the ballroom where the wedding was to be held. "There you are!" she cried. "I tried to call your cell phone. When you weren't answering I called Avery and she said you were running late."

"Yes. Sorry, Maddie. We're here now." She smiled brightly. "Tyler and Nick are going to help, so we can get over to the house and get ready."

"The photographer's coming at three," Maddie reminded her.

"I know," Kaelin said tightly.

It seemed like a shitload of decorations to Tyler, but he dutifully did as asked, setting out more floral centerpieces, the same pink and fuchsia and white flowers. Nick helped Kaelin drape masses of white tulle and little white lights around tables. Finally they had to set candles into each centerpiece and lay out little wrapped packages at each place setting.

They dimmed the lights and Kaelin studied the room. She sighed with relief. "It looks beautiful."

"Yeah." Tyler and Nick exchanged a grimace.

"Your mom would have my ass if it didn't," she said to him and he burst out laughing.

"I don't know," he said. "I think you've pretty much got her wrapped around your finger."

It was her turn to make a face. "*Not.*" She picked up empty boxes and stacked them.

"We'll get those," Nick said. "Are you done?"

"Yeah." She picked up her purse. "I still have to go home.

All my makeup and hair stuff is there. I didn't have time to pack it earlier."

"I'll just head over there now," Maddie said. "See you soon." With a wave she disappeared out the door, leaving the three of them alone in the vast empty ballroom.

Tyler set his hands on Kaelin's waist. She tried to pull back, but he held on. "I'm sorry, Kaelin. We shouldn't have all crashed like that."

She shrugged, avoiding eye contact. "Only to be expected when you stay up all night, I guess."

He looked down at her. Her jaw was pink and he rubbed a thumb over the whisker burn. She had dark circles under her tired eyes. "What else can we do?" he asked.

She shook her head. "Nothing. Thank you." She paused. "Really."

"I've heard if you put tea bags on your eyes it helps with the puffiness."

Her eyes flew open wide and met his. "My eyes are puffy?"

"Just trying to help."

She must have seen the laughter in his eyes, because her mouth slowly curved into a smile. "I look like hell, I know," she said. "And I have to pose for pictures."

"At least you don't have a black eye."

She touched her fingertips to his cheekbone. "It's barely noticeable today."

"Yeah. Whatever."

She sighed. "I better go pack a huge bag of makeup."

"You look beautiful."

"You do, Kaelin." Nick moved behind her and squeezed her shoulders. "It'll be fine. Go on, we'll finish cleaning up here."

She smiled at him over her shoulder and nodded. "Okay. I'll see you at the church, I guess."

They watched her walk out, her cute butt outlined by the snug, low-rise jeans. Tyler turned to Nick.

"Did we screw up big time, or what?" he asked.

The Visine, the tea bags and the heavy-duty concealer did seem to help. The several large cups of coffee she'd downed served to keep her alert, though her shaky hands were going to be pretty obvious as she carried her bouquet down the aisle ahead of Avery. Dammit.

What had she been thinking? Okay, sure, she'd wanted one wild night, but did she have to do it the night before her best friend got married? She closed her eyes, standing there in front of the full-length mirror in a Wirth guest room, then opened them again to study her reflection.

The bridesmaid dress was very nice, as bridesmaid dresses went. At least it wasn't pouffy and hideous, and powder pink was a good color for her. Strapless, like Avery's, the knee-length skirt was fuller, not straight, and a big satin bow tied around the waist. She held her arrangement of pink lilies, amaryllis, speckled green phalaenopsis orchids, pink dendrobium, and dusty pink calla lilies. Honeysuckle foliage trailed in a free-flowing cascade and she lifted the flowers to her nose to inhale their sweet scent. God, she hoped Avery liked them.

She sat on the bed to slip on the bronze shoes, sling backs with a pointy toe and an elegant heel. Okay. She was ready, on time and though maybe not looking and feeling her best, she'd have to do.

She left her room and knocked on Avery's door.

"Who is it?"

"Me. Kaelin."

"Come in."

She opened the door and walked in. Avery was still there alone, dressed, breathtakingly beautiful. She faced Kaelin and smiled. "You look gorgeous, Kaelin."

"Oh my god, so do you. So beautiful."

Avery literally glowed, her skin golden against the white dress. The dress did in fact look stunning on, fitted to Avery's curves, her small waist and slender hips. Her blonde hair sat on her head in a simple, gleaming updo and the long necklaces of pearls and rhinestones added sparkle to the dress in a sophisticated way.

"See what Scott gave me?" Avery tipped her head.

"The earrings?" Kaelin moved closer.

"Yes."

Ginormous diamonds studs winked at her from Avery's lobes. "Is that to make up for last night?" Kaelin asked with a smile.

Avery laughed. "I think he had these before then."

"You're not mad at him anymore?"

Avery sighed. "No. Everything worked out okay. Thanks again for your help. That Brent seems really nice."

"Ha!" Kaelin couldn't stop the word from exploding out of her mouth. "He gave me a speeding ticket today!"

"What!" Avery gaped at her. "Is that why you were running late?"

"Er...yes." Kaelin swallowed. "Forget that. Where's Maddie?"

"Right here," she said from behind them. They turned to watch her, in her identical pink dress, cross the room. Maddie and Kaelin helped fasten the pink orchids into Avery's blonde hair, then Avery added a little highlighter to Kaelin's face. "You look a little washed out," she said. "That's better."

Two hours of sleep would do that to you. Two hours of sleep and six hours of wicked hot sex. *Don't go there.*

When a knock on the door sounded, Kaelin opened it to see Mrs. Wirth standing there. Her blonde hair also shone in an elegant up-do and more diamonds sparkled at her ears. She, too, wore pink, but a deeper rose pink that flattered her creamy complexion and her toned figure.

"Oh, Kaelin." Mrs. Wirth smiled and tipped her head to one side. "You look beautiful."

"Thanks."

"Is Avery ready? Can I come in?"

Kaelin turned and cocked an eyebrow at Avery who nodded. Kaelin let Mrs. Wirth in. She stopped and lifted her hands to her mouth, regarding her daughter.

"Avery. Honey." Tears trembled on her mascaraed lashes. Hopefully it was waterproof. Weddings had a way of bringing on a few tears.

Mrs. With touched a fingertip to her eyes. "You look absolutely gorgeous, honey. That dress is incredible."

"I thought you might be disappointed." Avery looked down at herself.

"Oh my goodness, how could I be disappointed? You look so elegant and glamorous. It's totally you."

Now Avery's eyes got all glossy and she and her mom hugged.

After innumerable posed photographs in the Wirth back yard in front of Mrs. Wirth's rose garden, the limo took them to the church.

"He'd better be there," Avery muttered as they neared the church. Kaelin shot her a startled glance.

"Are you worried about that?" she asked.

"Not really." Avery grinned. "I just don't want anything else to go wrong."

"It's going to be fine." Surely to god nothing else could go wrong.

They entered the church through the side door and waited upstairs as guests entered, listening to the faint strains of guitar and piano. Kaelin faced her friend, putting all her own crazy thoughts and memories out of her head for her friend's big moment. She smiled at her. "Almost time."

"I'm ready." Avery smiled, her lips shiny, eyes shinier.

Tyler appeared in the door. "Okay," he said. "We just seated Scott's parents and Mom and Dad. Time to go, Sis."

"Oh." Avery took a breath. "Okay."

"Sure you want to go through with it?" Tyler asked.

"Tyler!"

"Just kidding. Don't hit me with that bouquet, you could kill someone with that. It weighs a freakin' ton."

"It does not."

Avery's cascade of flowers was three times the size of her bridesmaids'. And this was keeping it simple. Ha.

The musicians changed to Vivaldi's Guitar Concerto in D Major and Maddie went down the aisle first. Kaelin followed her, hoping her hands weren't shaking too badly, a smile pasted on her face. When she passed Nick, seated right on the aisle, and caught his eye, his reassuring smile, she relaxed. A little. Tried not to think about him naked. No. Not now. Her hands started shaking again.

Tyler stood at the front of the sanctuary, gorgeous in a

141

black tux. He, too, caught her eye, but instead of reassuring her, the wicked glint in his eyes had her almost hyperventilating.

They all turned to watch Avery come down the aisle, radiant and beautiful. The ceremony was mercifully short, though Kaelin wondered if she actually fell asleep standing up for a few moments, it seemed so short, and then it was done and Avery and Scott were man and wife.

They turned to walk back up the aisle, Hardeep holding out his arm for Kaelin. And then something weird happened. The pianist and guitar player finished their song, the church went quiet, and then strong, beating guitar chords throbbed through the church. The music sounded familiar... Kaelin frowned, trying to place it. The chords beat on and on, and just as she realized what it was and turned wide-eyed to Avery, the Black Eyed Peas started singing "I Got a Feeling".

Avery grinned.

She'd planned this! Kaelin laughed out loud, caught the eye of Tyler, who was smiling too, then she took Hardeep's arm. Avery waved them to go back up the aisle and so they did, moving to the uplifting beat of the music as it picked up tempo. Kaelin got a glimpse of the shocked look on Dr. and Mrs. Wirth's faces, in contrast to everyone else in the church who seemed highly amused. Just at the door to the vestibule, Hardeep twirled her in a dance move and she laughed again, turned to watch Maddie and Tyler coming, smiling and laughing, and Tyler gave Maddie a spin too. Then Avery and Scott danced up the aisle in some moves they'd obviously practiced, laughing and looking so triumphant and happy, the jubilant music making everyone's spirits lift, making everyone smile, and there could not have been a happier, more celebratory end to the traditional ceremony. It was indeed going to be a good night.

Chapter Eleven

The dinner and speeches were over. The cupcakes had been handed out by the bride and groom. The happy couple had danced their first dance, and Tyler had had several beers. It was a pretty good night.

His mom had driven him a little nuts with all the photographs, but overall she was too busy socializing to have time to bug him, and he'd actually enjoyed talking to some of his relatives—aunts, uncles, cousins—who were interested in his life in Chicago and his new business, and it was cool to talk to them too and hear about their lives, to reminisce a little. The wedding was almost...fun.

He looked around for Nick and Kaelin and found them together. On the dance floor. Talking and smiling at each other as they moved to the slow song. Tyler leaned back in the chair and lifted his glass to his mouth, watching them.

He hadn't had much time to think about last night. After being so rudely awoken that morning—okay, not rudely, but abruptly—they'd been racing around all day getting things ready, then getting pictures taken, then the wedding, then more pictures.

He should be shocked as hell by Kaelin's behavior last night. Sweet little Kaelin, the town sweetheart. He wanted to laugh, thinking about what people would think if they knew.

His eyes roved over the guests—his parents, who loved Kaelin and thought she could paint a rainbow in the sky. Paul Bickford, the town's most prominent lawyer, his dad's best friend and coincidentally, Kaelin's boss. Reverend McTavish, who'd performed the ceremony. What would they all think if they knew the truth about Kaelin?

His mouth twisted into a wry smile. They'd probably still love her. In fact, they probably wouldn't even believe it.

Was he shocked? Somehow, no. He had complicated feelings about what had happened last night, that was for damn sure, but shock wasn't really in there. Amazement, arousal definitely, admiration for her guts at going after what she'd clearly wanted so deep-down inside, and even something that felt like...gratitude.

Maybe because she hadn't been shocked. Not at what she herself had done. She'd wanted it. But she hadn't been shocked at him and Nick. And for some reason, that tugged at his heart and made him feel something huge and warm and... Jesus. He sat up straight. It felt like those old feelings he'd had for Kaelin back in high school, especially that last summer before he'd moved away, that summer they'd spent all that time together and he'd gotten to know her better and...

The summer he'd deliberately hurt her because he knew she was having the same feelings for him, and he knew there was no fucking way he was anywhere near good enough for her. The town sweetheart and the town asshole? Not likely. Not to mention she was two years older than him and his big sister's best friend.

He drained the last of the beer and sighed. He'd been having such a good time, why did he have to start thinking about crap like that? He should just drink more beer and keep himself busy so he didn't start thinking things that would get him into trouble. Like he always did.

Kaelin smiled at Nick. She'd been a little nervous about how she was going to feel with him and Tyler today after what had happened. But as always with Nick, she just felt comfortable and warm. He didn't make her feel like the town slut even after what she'd done. And strangely, when she examined her feelings, she didn't feel like the town slut anyway.

Sure it had been wicked. Wicked fun. Wicked sexy. Something she'd remember for the rest of her life. 'Cause that would never happen again.

Only, was she ever again going to be satisfied with vanilla missionary sex with the lights out, like Brent had wanted? It hadn't satisfied her. It had driven her crazy with frustration and a deep, hungry yearning that she couldn't find the nerve to tell him about.

"What's wrong?" Nick asked, looking down at her, his hands on her waist, hers linked around his neck.

She smiled. "Nothing."

"Regrets?"

She shook her head. "No. Not the way you mean." She peered up at him. "You never told Tyler we kept in touch, did you?"

"No. I told you that in my emails."

She nodded. "Thank you." She'd asked him not to, but she'd never been sure if he'd kept that from Tyler.

"Did your ex-fiancé really give you a speeding ticket this morning?"

Her smile disappeared. "Yes." She frowned. "He really did."

"Jerk."

"That's the thing. He's not a jerk. He's a really nice guy."

"Sounds exciting."

She eyed him and saw the understanding in his eyes.

"Nice guys are boring," he said.

"You're a nice guy."

"Gee, thanks."

She laughed. "No! That's not what I meant! You're not boring! My god, how can you think that!"

"I'm boring compared to Tyler."

She shook her head slowly. "No. You're different, that's true. But not boring. Never."

"Thanks."

They shared another smile.

"Why'd you break up with him?"

She blinked at him.

"Brent," he clarified.

"Oh." She dropped her head to his shoulder briefly then looked back up at him. "Because he was boring."

Nick grinned. "See."

She nibbled her bottom lip. "I never realized how much I wanted something...more. Something wilder."

"You think you're gonna find that here? In Mapleglen?"

She stared at him, his question reminding her of their conversation last night. "What are you saying?"

He lifted one shoulder. The song came to an end and they stopped moving, stepped apart. "I don't know. I guess I'm saying last night was special. And after that, are you going to be satisfied with some other guy like Brent?"

"Maybe I just needed to get that out of my system."

He tipped his head to one side. "Maybe."

Tyler appeared beside them. "My turn," he said, elbowing Nick out of the way. Nick just grinned and moved away and Kaelin turned to Tyler.

"Hey," he said. "Great job on the wedding."

"Thanks."

The music started again, the tinkling opening notes of "Babe" by Styx. Tyler took her in his arms and she moved against him. He was a couple of inches taller than Nick, leaner, but just as strong. She couldn't help but smile as she thought about how she would have reacted to this in high school, slow dancing with Tyler Wirth. God, she would have been so tongue-tied and intimidated. Now she'd slept with him. Lord. That flippy, fluttering feeling down low inside her returned. "And thanks for your help this afternoon." She had to keep things cool tonight. Even though she couldn't help thinking about Tyler and Nick's hotel room, just a few floors above them, with that big king-size bed and...

Oh. She took a breath. Oh dear.

"You helped us out last night," he said.

She drew back and stared at him. "Help?" Did he mean she helped him and Nick? That was...

"At the police station."

"Oh! Oh yeah. Well." She shrugged.

Tyler's hands slid lower on her hips, his fingertips resting on the curve of her butt. Heat pooled between her thighs at the sexy touch.

"Um. So. Speaking of last night. Do you often take the blame for things that aren't your fault?" she asked him.

His thick gold brows drew together. "What do you mean?"

He moved them out of the path of a tipsy couple with gentle

147

pressure on one of her hips.

"I mean, like last night, when you tried to take the blame for stealing the fire truck."

"We didn't steal it. We were just taking it for a ride. We were going to bring it back."

She arched a brow. "Remember when you totaled your parents' car? When you were seventeen?"

His eyes grew wary. "Yeah."

She watched him, and he watched her back, moving to the music on the dimly lit dance floor, surrounded by twinkling white lights and flowers, and vocal harmonies and words about love and courage and strength. Her fingers moved on the warm skin of his neck above the collar of his shirt. "You didn't do it," she said quietly.

He bent his head closer to hers. "Sure I did. Got in a shitload of trouble over it too."

"Avery did it." She met his blue gaze. "I know she did it. Why did you take the blame?"

He swallowed. His eyes shifted away from her, then back. "She'd been drinking that night." His voice hardened. "She shouldn't have been driving, the stupid idiot, but thankfully she didn't kill anyone else. Or herself."

Tyler apparently had wrapped the car around a tree and walked away from it. But Kaelin had always known the truth, though it was another of those secrets that was never spoken of.

"She came running home in a big panic. She would have been in way worse trouble than I was," he said gruffly. "I was sober. So I walked back to where she'd crashed and told everyone I was driving. Everyone just chalked it up to me being stupid and reckless."

Her heart expanded in her chest until she thought she couldn't breathe, and she leaned in closer and tightened her arms around him in a squeeze. "You're not such a bad boy," she whispered in his ear.

He hugged her back, his arms crushingly tight around her, his face pressed to her hair. "Yes, I am. Don't even think otherwise. Please."

She didn't understand that, didn't know what he meant, only knew that she was very likely falling in love with him all over again.

Which scared the hell out of her.

Margot wanted to slap Jean Griffin.

She stared coolly back at the other woman. Jean loved to gossip, and even though she apologized for telling Margot what she just had, Margot knew she took great delight in doing it.

"Les works the front desk here at the hotel," Jean continued gleefully, all but rubbing her hands. "He was working the night shift last night. That's how he saw it."

She had to shut this rumor down, but how? Her mind spun in circles. She just didn't even know what to say to Jean. Boys will be boys? How about that. No? Her stomach churned. When Ken heard this he was going to flip. After what had happened ten years ago? God.

But she pasted on her usual smile, that one she was so good at after all these years. "Oh for heaven's sake," she said lightly. "Has he nothing better to do with his time than spread silly rumors like that?"

"I just thought you should know. Before someone else tells you. You know how some people like to gossip." And Jean moved on to talk to some others. Probably to spread the rumor, the silly bitch.

Margot bit her lip and searched the wedding crowd for her husband. The room looked lovely, though she would have added more flower arrangements and she knew that Forget Me Not Florists had a gorgeous backdrop that looked like a starry sky, which she'd seen at the Bickfords' daughter's wedding. It was lovely, but Kaelin had gently reminded her that Avery wanted just a few simple decorations.

There was Ken. Should she tell him? Or should she take a chance that nobody else would be interested in such gossip and it would just die away? She downed the last of the champagne in her glass, now too warm to really taste good.

And where was Tyler, the subject of the gossip? Her eyes roamed the room again. Tyler sat alone behind the head table, leaning back in his chair looking all handsome and lazy and...alone. This would be a good chance to talk to him, to talk about what had happened, perhaps to prepare him for the rumor that might be circulating even now.

"Margot." She turned. Ken stood there, tight lipped. Shit. She closed her eyes.

"You heard."

"What the hell was he doing?" Ken barked. "Does he have no sense whatsoever? He leaves town with a huge scandal hanging over his head—"

"Nobody knew about that," she interrupted automatically.

"We knew about it! You'd think he could keep his pants zipped for one weekend, for Chrissake. And with Nick again..." Hs voice trailed off and he glared at her. As if it was her fault.

"I'm sure it's nothing," she began, but he was furious, and she had to admit, she felt a small frisson of annoyance, too, that this had to happen at Avery's wedding, when she'd had all those hopes for how this was going to go. Instead, typical Tyler, he'd come home and gotten in trouble again. She had to admit, for a moment she shared that same thought—could he not just have been on his best behavior for one weekend?

She watched Tyler finish his beer, rise out of his chair and cross the dance floor. He stopped beside Nick and Kaelin and looked down at her with such warm affection, Margot's heart stopped.

Dear god. Not Kaelin. Her fingers flew to her mouth.

Fear and dread gnawing at her insides, she continued watching as Tyler and Kaelin moved together, dancing to the slow song in an intimate hold, body pressed to body, her arms looped around his neck, gazing up at him, his hands low on her hips. Emotion swelled inside Margot, a complex mix of joy to see Tyler smiling like that with such tenderness and happiness, fear that he was going to break Kaelin's sweet heart, and longing for something she couldn't even name.

"I want him out of here," Ken snapped. "Before he ruins Avery's wedding."

She turned to her husband with dismay. "No. Ken. Not tonight. I'm sure it was nothing, truly."

This couldn't be happening all over again. She'd buried her anger and resentment toward her husband for how harshly he'd reacted last time with Tyler. Or, she *thought* she'd buried her anger and resentment. It was starting to seep up to the surface, resurrected by her disappointment that this wedding wasn't apparently going to be the family reunion she'd longed for. She didn't want to blame Ken for it all. Lord knew, she'd done her part, enabling Ken in his authoritarian discipline, trying to make everything look good on the outside, trying to make their family appear all perfect and loving, when the reality was, things were a big mess. She'd always thought she was doing the right thing, keeping Ken happy, trying desperately to keep their family together, but now... She pressed a hand to her aching heart. She did not want to live this all over again.

"It doesn't matter if it was nothing!" he said, the words stiff and tight. "What matters is that people are talking about it!"

"Oh, for—" She curled her fingers into her palms. "You don't know that!"

"Of course I know it! You've heard it, I've heard it, we might as well get up to the microphone and announce it to the whole wedding."

"It doesn't matter." But it did matter. To him. She sighed. Maybe she could talk to Tyler alone. This time she'd handle things, and she'd handle it differently. "I'll talk to him."

She set off across the dance floor, her high heels clicking on the parquet floor. She paused beside Tyler and Kaelin. "Tyler."

Tyler and Kaelin moved apart to look at Tyler's mom, standing beside them on the dance floor. Her cheeks were red, her eyes snapped and she glared at him. Was she angry because they were dancing together?

"What, Mom?"

Mrs. Wirth glanced at Kaelin and frowned. "What are you doing, dear?" she asked.

"Um...dancing."

"Never mind." Mrs. Wirth waved a hand. "Tyler, I need to talk to you. Alone."

He lifted one eyebrow and released Kaelin, the song ending just then anyway.

"Go on," Kaelin said with a smile, though a feeling of dread crawled over her skin. She watched them walk away, Mrs.

Wirth's posture stiff, her steps in her high heels urgent, Tyler's gait loose and easy as he sauntered beside her. They moved to one side of the ballroom and were almost immediately joined by Tyler's dad, who folded his arms across his chest.

Nick came up behind her and set his hands on her waist. "What's going on?" he murmured.

"I don't know. But she looks pissed."

Nick sighed. "She's always pissed at Tyler about something."

"What on earth could he have done? We were just dancing. You don't think she could possibly be upset about him dancing with me, do you?"

"Not out of the question." They watched her gesturing, looking as if she was nearly yelling, though they couldn't hear anything from where they were. "But it looks like a little more than that to me."

"Um. Yeah." Her heart rose to her throat as she watched. She tipped her head to look up at Nick over her shoulder. "What should we do?"

He watched them unhappily.

Tyler leaned against the wall, looking careless and relaxed. He flashed a smile, but even from across the room, Kaelin could see how phony it was. Then he straightened. Stared at his parents. Said something to them. Mr. Wirth shook his head violently, and gestured toward the door.

"Dear god," Kaelin breathed. "Are they kicking him out?"

"Can't be."

Tyler stood there for a few seconds longer, and Mrs. Wirth lifted a hand. This time it wasn't entirely clear if she was pleading with him or telling to get out, but Tyler took a step back, then turned and started toward the nearest exit from the ballroom.

Now Kaelin turned fully to peer up at Nick. "What...?"

"I'll go after him."

"I'm coming too."

"Kaelin..." He paused, then said, "Yeah. You come too."

They hurried out of the wedding, now a song by Beyoncé getting everyone grooving on the dance floor. They passed Aunt Mona shaking her double Ds and exchanged a *yikes* glance.

Tyler was still at the elevator and they caught up to him just as the doors slid open. He glared at them. "What the hell are you doing?" he snarled.

They stepped in with him and Nick pushed the button for their floor.

"What the hell are *you* doing?" he asked Tyler back, his voice mild. "What's going on, buddy?"

Tyler scowled. "Nothing."

"What was your mom talking to you about?" Kaelin asked. She tried to take his hand, but he jerked it away. A flash of pain seared through her at his rejection. Oh boy. Once again, just because *she* was developing feelings for *him,* completely inappropriate feelings, didn't mean that he was for her. She pushed away the hurt.

"Nothing."

"Clearly it wasn't nothing. For Chrissake, man, just tell us."

The doors opened and they walked down the hall to the room. Tyler slid his keycard in out and out and opened the door, then pushed into the dark room.

Kaelin followed. The bed had been made and the room straightened. You'd never know what they'd done in that bed last night. Her stomach clenched and her fingers curled into her palms.

Tyler looked at her. "Go back to the wedding, Kaelin. You shouldn't be up here."

Her mouth fell open and she gazed back at him. "I just want to make sure you're okay."

"Of course I'm okay! Jesus Christ." He ran a hand through his hair and gave a harsh laugh. "You don't need to worry about me."

But she *was* worried about him. His cheekbones wore a flush of anger and his blue eyes glittered. His beautiful mouth was a thin line across his face.

"Seriously, Kaelin. Get the hell out of here."

His words were like a slap and she jerked back.

"Tyler." Nick's voice cut through the tension. "What the fuck?"

"You want to know what's going on?" The rage on Tyler's face almost scared her and she took a step back, feeling as if a knife was turning in her chest. "Fine. I'll tell you. There's a rumor going around about me. About us." He looked at Nick and gestured with his hand between them. Nick frowned. "About last night. About how we were making out with some slutty chick in the lobby of the hotel and took her back to our room."

Kaelin gasped and covered her mouth with her hands. Her eyes went wide and her head spun.

"That's right," Tyler said, voice still steely, turning back to her. "Apparently the front desk clerk was getting an eyeful. But he didn't recognize you. So nobody apparently knows it's you. And you'd better damn well hope it stays that way. Which is why I'm telling you, get the hell out of here now. Before this gets worse."

Her chest burning, her throat aching, she just stood there.

155

"Oh my god."

"Your sweet and innocent reputation will be ruined," he continued nastily. "You also better hope after seeing you in the same clothes as last night that Cop Boy doesn't put two and two together and get four. Or should I say three. Ha."

"Fuck." Nick sat down heavily on the side of the bed. "Fuck."

"We did that already," Tyler said, heading for the mini fridge. "Several times."

Kaelin looked at Nick, who held his head in his hands. Then he looked at her. "Kaelin. I'm so sorry."

Sorry? Maybe she was stupid, but what was to be sorry for? If whoever saw them hadn't recognized her, nobody was going to figure it out. Nobody would guess in a million years.

"Your parents don't know it was me," she repeated.

"Not a clue. My mom thinks we picked up a hooker or a dancer from the Pussy Cat Palace or something. They're completely mortified and pissed off. So mad in fact, that they told me to leave before I ruin Avery's wedding." Bitterness edged his tone. He popped the top off a beer and gulped down half of it.

"Oh for god's sake," she said. She rubbed her forehead, trying to think. "You're an adult. What you do is your business."

"Not when the front desk clerk at the Red Maple Inn sees me and starts telling the whole town. And embarrassing my poor parents. Jesus." He tipped his head back. "I knew I shouldn't have come back here."

Silence loomed around them. Kaelin didn't know what to do, what to say. "I feel like I'm the one who should apologize," she whispered, twisting her fingers together in front of her. "It was me who instigated that. It was my idea." She tipped her head to one side and regarded Tyler miserably. "This time it was me who got you in trouble."

"Oh for shit's sake," he growled. "Don't be stupid. I get myself in trouble. All the fucking time."

Nick closed his eyes and tipped his head back. "You know, I'm getting sick of that story," he said.

"What?" Tyler glared at him.

Afraid they were going to start a fistfight, Kaelin took a step toward them.

"Never mind," Nick said. "Kaelin, I'll go back down with you."

"I'm not going back," she said heavily. "I can't go back."

"Nobody knows it was you," Tyler reminded her. "Your reputation is safe, babe."

"I'm not worried about that," she said, though in fact, she was. A little. Her boss was down there. Could she get fired if someone found out? Dear lord, that entire law firm was so conservative and straitlaced, they probably didn't know the meaning of ménage à trois without looking it up in a French dictionary. They would totally freak out if they knew.

It was her business, just like she'd told Tyler. And she didn't regret a second of it.

"I'm not going back unless you both come," she said.

"Oh Jesus." Tyler finished the beer and smacked it down on the desk. "I'm not going back. Mom was right. It's Avery's wedding and I don't want to ruin it for her. And to think..." He passed a hand over his eyes. "I was actually having a good time for a while there."

Her heart squeezed and she took another step forward. "She wanted you there, Tyler. Avery did."

He sighed. "Well, I was there. And now I'm gone. It's done. The wedding's almost over anyway. First thing in the morning, we're checking out of here and getting our asses back to Chicago."

Nick said nothing, his mouth pursed. Then he shook his head.

"What?" Tyler demanded.

"You gotta face your parents, man," he said. "This is never going to end if you don't."

"Face them? How? Why? What am I supposed to say to them? What difference would it possibly make? I can't defend myself to them."

Kaelin gulped. Yeah, what was he going to tell them? It was true, they'd had a threesome last night in their hotel room. Couldn't really get out of that.

"I don't understand why they're so upset about it," she said, her voice still coming out in a near whisper through her tight throat. "Like I said, it's your business. Who cares if you have threesomes every night of the week?"

Nick and Tyler exchanged a glance that confused her with its angst. What was going on?

"You know how they are," Tyler said, not meeting her eyes.

"Yes, but...well. I suppose it is a little shocking."

Tyler laughed. "Kaelin Daume. Are you telling me threesomes are common in Mapleglen?"

"No." He was back to his mocking, cynical self, and her stomach cramped. "I'm not saying that. I guess you're right. Your mom and dad were always worried about what people thought."

"And so are you."

She met his gaze, her heart thudding painfully in her chest, her legs shaking.

"Aren't you?" he challenged.

She bit her bottom lip to stop it from trembling, looked at Nick, who surged up off the bed.

"Enough, Tyler. You're being an asshole again." Nick came at her and wrapped her up in a hug and she leaned into him, her eyes burning, throat paralyzed. "Kaelin. It's okay. I'm sorry about all this."

"You don't need to be sorry," she mumbled into his shoulder. "I'm the one who should be sorry. But I don't know how to fix it."

"You don't need to fix it." Nick glanced at Tyler. "It's Tyler's problem to fix. He just doesn't want to."

Chapter Twelve

They were actually in the car, packed up and ready to leave town, when Nick brought it up again. Damn him.

"You should go say goodbye to Avery, at least," Nick said quietly from the passenger seat. "If not Kaelin."

Tyler slid his sunglasses onto his nose. It was later than he'd wanted to leave, but they'd both crashed and slept late. They'd grabbed breakfast in the hotel coffee shop and packed up, but it was noon already.

"They're busy opening gifts at the house," he said. "Let's just go."

"Tyler."

He sighed and stared straight ahead.

"You know you have to deal with this."

"Why?"

"Because this chip on your shoulder is wrecking your life. Fuck." Nick turned his head away and looked out the side window for a moment. "Look at you. We've been arguing about the Healthy Solutions account. You want the money and don't care about the ethics. You want the prestige of having them for a client."

"What the hell does that have to do with anything?" Tyler asked. "It'll make a difference. You can't deny that."

"We don't need them," Nick said. "We'll have other opportunities to demonstrate your brilliance, to make money. And I'm not sure I want to be associated with a company who scams people."

Tyler tightened his mouth. "Buyer beware."

"Don't you see? You only want them for a client because of how it will look good for us. You're no different than your parents, for Chrissake."

Tyler felt everything inside him shift as he processed Nick's words. That was not true. He wanted to shout out a denial. But he couldn't. Shit. *Shit.*

"You push away people who care for you. I know how you feel about Kaelin. How you've always felt about her. And you hurt her feelings."

"She knew that was just one night."

"That's not what I'm talking about. And you know it."

Yeah. He did. Guilt washed through him. He still stared out the windshield, still parked in the hotel parking lot. "There's no fucking way we could ever have anything," he growled. "She's way too good for that."

Nick heaved an exaggerated sigh. "Do you have any idea how insulting that is?"

Tyler turned and squinted at him through his dark lenses. "What are you talking about?"

"She's too good for you. But I'm not. What does that say about me?"

Tyler stared at Nick wordlessly, mouth open, then closing. He swallowed. His brain ran in circles. "It's not like that," he said. "It's different. It's not an insult."

"Forget it." Nick waved a hand. "If you go back there and try to talk to them, what do you think will happen?"

"Nothing! That's the point! Nothing will change!"

"No, I mean, what's the worst thing that could happen? What the hell are you so afraid of?"

Tyler gripped the steering wheel so tight his fingers hurt. His head felt as if it was going to explode, so much pressure built up inside him. His heart hammered and stomach churned. What *was* he afraid of?

He knew. He'd always known. He closed his eyes. Gritted his teeth.

"Tyler." Nick's voice was softer.

"I'm afraid—" His voice cracked. Embarrassed, he turned away. "Fuck. Fuck you, Nick."

"Yeah, yeah."

"I'm afraid..." He swallowed hard. "If I tell them the truth, I'm afraid it won't make any difference." The words were wrenched out of him painfully, like ripping a hole in his gut. "They still won't love me, even if they know the truth."

There. It was out. He'd spoken it aloud. He couldn't look at Nick.

Nick's hand landed on his knee. "You gotta face it, man," he said again, quietly. "You gotta live with yourself. Thinking that is eating you alive. You have to tell them. You have to try to move on."

"I can't tell them everything. Some of it's not mine to tell." He thought of Kaelin confronting him about the wrecked car when he was seventeen. He couldn't betray his sister by telling his parents the truth about that.

"Not all of it, no."

"I tried to tell them. They didn't believe me."

"You didn't try. Like always, you just let them blame you and never said a goddamn word."

162

Tyler bent his head.

"You wanted them to have stuff to hate you about, didn't you?"

He said nothing, but he knew the truth of it. He'd never felt he could live up to their expectations. So he made sure that he didn't.

"How's that working for you?" Nick asked dryly, breaking the tension. Tyler choked out a laugh.

"I can't do it."

"I'm with you."

"I'm not sure that helps." Tyler lifted his head and gave Nick a rueful smile. "You want me to tell them about us?"

"If you want to, I'm fine with it." Nick held his gaze steadily.

"Fuck, man," Tyler whispered. "You fucking kill me."

"Yeah, I know. I'm fine if you don't tell them, too. Your choice."

Tyler felt as if his guts were being ripped out of him. "Fuck," he said again.

With a smile on her face but a heavy heart, Kaelin watched Avery open another lovely gift. She'd admired the gifts, helped Avery keep track of who'd given what, fetched more drinks and coffee for the family members who had gathered in the Wirth living room the day after the wedding. It wasn't a large gathering, and Tyler's absence was very conspicuous.

Even though he wasn't there, the tension in the room was palpable. Dr. and Mrs. Wirth looked as if they hadn't had much sleep. They barely spoke to each other—in fact, they barely looked at each other. Even Avery, glowing and happy, had a glimmer of worry in her eyes. Again, Kaelin and she didn't

163

speak about what had happened the night before, and Kaelin wasn't even sure if Avery knew anything about it.

Secrets. So many secrets. Probably many she didn't even know about in this complicated family.

She sighed, remembering Tyler's anguish the night before. Both his parents' reaction and his seemed a little out of proportion about the whole thing, though she had to admit maybe she'd feel differently if she'd been identified as the "hooker" they'd taken up to their room.

She rolled her eyes, earning a puzzled glance from Avery. "You don't like these candlesticks?" Avery asked.

"Oh no! They're lovely."

Avery nodded and packed them back into the tissue.

She'd rolled her eyes because she was suddenly so tired of worrying what people thought, and annoyed with Dr. and Mrs. Wirth's insistence on maintaining the perfect image. All through the wedding plans she'd had to battle with that, to keep what Avery wanted in the forefront, not what her mother wanted or thought they should have. She was exhausted from all of it.

And then the front door opened and closed.

"Can you see who that is, Kaelin dear?" Mrs. Wirth called from the kitchen.

"Of course."

And just as she arrived at the French doors, she came face-to-face with Tyler, Nick following right behind him. They stopped and stared at each other.

"Hey," he finally said. "Just stopped in on our way out of town to...uh..."

His hair was going every which way, he hadn't shaved and his usual devilish smile was absent. His gray T-shirt hugged his wide chest and abs, and faded jeans, the ones he'd dragged on the other night to go searching for munchies for them, sat low on his hips, low enough to reveal a thin strip of golden skin between the hem of his T-shirt and the jeans. Nick's dark jeans and black shirt were just as sexy, but in a different way.

"Come in," Kaelin said.

"Hey, Tyler, come see what we got," Avery called from where she sat in an armchair. "I thought you two weren't coming."

"Yeah. Well..."

The smooth-talking devil seemed at a loss for words today. Worry gnawed at Kaelin's tummy and she exchanged a glance with Nick that, for once, didn't reassure her. He didn't look much better than Tyler, tired and quiet. Though Nick was always quieter than Tyler.

"I wanted to say goodbye to you. And Scott," Tyler said. "When are you leaving on your honeymoon?"

"Tonight. We drive to St. Louis and fly out from there."

"Three weeks in Europe. Sounds amazing."

She smiled up at him. "Yeah. I'm excited."

"Where are Mom and Dad?" Tyler asked, looking around.

"Mom's making more coffee. Not sure where Dad is."

"He's in the den watching golf," Scott said, walking into the room. "Hey, Tyler, Nick."

A muscle twitched in Tyler's jaw. "I guess I'll go find him. Need to talk to them both."

Kaelin met Nick's eyes. He pursed his lips and folded his arms across his broad chest, then sighed as Tyler disappeared. She moved closer to him. "What's going on?" she asked him quietly.

"He has something he wants to talk to them about."

She squinted at him unhappily. "Is it about last night?"

"No. Well, sort of. But it's not about you. Don't worry."

"I *am* worried. I don't understand what's going on. I mean, I do, but it all seems so blown out of proportion."

Nick blew out a breath and rubbed his nearly shaved head. "Maybe you should know about it. You were kind of involved."

"Know about what?" Confusion swirled inside her.

"Come in the kitchen." He led the way to the now empty kitchen. Coffee dripped into the carafe of the coffeemaker on the counter. It smelled dark and delicious. The door to the den off the kitchen was open and they heard Tyler's voice, but couldn't hear what he was saying.

Nick turned to her, and spoke quietly. "You know that night you walked in on us? Ten years ago?"

Her stomach swooped. "Yes."

Nick closed his eyes. Then opened them. He looked as if someone were stabbing him in the stomach. "After you showed up, Tracy uh...changed her mind about what we were doing. She wanted to go home. I think she freaked out that someone else saw her like that."

Kaelin didn't know what to say to that. Freaked out was probably a mild way to describe how Tracy had felt, although she'd been enjoying herself pretty well up to that point as Kaelin stood there hiding behind the door, watching and listening. "I'm sorry," she said stiffly, wondering if they blamed her for ending their fun.

Nick shook his head. "Don't fucking apologize, Kaelin," he growled. "It wasn't your fault. Tracy was kind of...psycho. If only we'd known that before. We were young and stupid and horny, what can I say. It seemed like a good idea at the time."

"Really?" She searched his face. "Did it really seem like a good idea, Nick?" Remembered hurt pulsed inside her.

Shame crossed over Nick's face and he dropped his gaze for a moment. "I'm sorry, Kaelin."

She nodded stiffly.

"Anyway, she went running home and I guess she was so paranoid that you were going to tell people what happened, she told her parents that..." Nick paused. Swallowed. "She told her parents we'd raped her."

Kaelin's jaw nearly smacked the counter she fell against. "What!"

He nodded, swiped a hand over his eyes. "She told them we'd tied her up and took turns having sex with her. It was a fucking nightmare. Her parents called both our parents. Thank Christ they didn't call the cops, although they wanted to."

"But you said nothing happened after that."

"Nothing did. We'd barely touched her and we for sure hadn't had sex at that point. Other than a little making out."

"Well, you *should* have called the cops! If nothing happened, they would have proved it."

"Oh, Kaelin, think about what you just said. We're talking Dr. and Mrs. Wirth here."

"Oh lord." She rubbed her mouth. They would not have wanted the police involved, and they sure wouldn't have wanted the entire city to know about it. "What happened?"

"Dr. Wirth paid off Tracy's family to keep quiet about it. I don't know how much he gave them, but it was a lot. My folks didn't have that kind of money, but they had a whole different attitude. I told them nothing happened and they believed me. We could have gone to the police and they would have supported me, even though it would have been a helluva mess."

She nodded, hand still to her mouth, her stomach boiling, head spinning. "I gather Tyler's parents weren't quite so supportive."

Nick snorted. "The stupid asshole didn't even try to explain what happened. They were so furious they kicked him out of the house."

Kaelin slumped against the counter. This was unbelievable. Her eyes stung and she blinked rapidly. "They did? He was only seventeen."

"Almost eighteen, but yeah. We were leaving for college in the fall anyway. It was all arranged, except Tyler's parents refused to pay, other than the tuition they'd already paid. They basically kicked him out and cut him off, for what he'd done."

"He didn't do anything!"

"You believe it," Nick said slowly.

"Of course I believe it! You two would never rape someone!"

"Sshh."

She hadn't even realized her voice was rising. She took a breath, tried to calm down.

"What did he do? I know he went to college."

"He lived with me, remember?"

Yeah, she remembered that. But...

"I had a little apartment off campus. My parents helped out, as much as they could. Tyler worked two part-time jobs while he was going to school. Didn't sleep much. Worked all summer, every year. He did it on his own."

She pressed a hand to her stomach, all tight and quivery, turned her gaze to him. "You love him, don't you?"

He held her gaze, eyes steady as usual. "Yeah. I do."

She nodded her head several times, hand still pressed to her stomach. "I was with you Friday night," she said. "Yes, you tied me up, but only because I asked you to. And Tyler said I had to be untied before we..."

Nick nodded. "Yeah. That's his thing. He'll never take a chance on that again. A chance that someone could accuse him of forcing her."

"I don't believe he would ever do that," she said fiercely. "Or you. God! His parents are—" She glanced at the den, where the voices were getting louder. "Is that what he's talking to them about?"

"Yeah. Probably finally trying to tell them nothing happened that night."

"I know she was there of her own free will!" Kaelin cried. "I was there! I saw it!"

"Well, you didn't see much..."

"I saw more than you realize," she said grimly. "Oh god, Nick. Why is he doing this?"

"Because he has to get past this somehow. Last night, his parents thought history was repeating itself. When they heard that rumor, they believed Tyler and I had done the same thing, lured some helpless girl to our room and took advantage of her. That's why they were so furious. They let him come home for the wedding..."

"*Let him come home!*" she cried, almost beside herself. "Dear god!" All these years she'd blamed him for never coming home to visit.

"And then he does the same thing again."

"This is insane!" Then she focused on Nick. "Why didn't you ever tell me this? My god, Nick!"

"He asked me not to." He held her gaze steadily. "Just like you asked me not to tell him we'd kept in touch."

She looked wildly around. Tyler was in there trying to tell his parents he wasn't the devil in disguise they thought he was.

169

The raised voices told her it wasn't going well. It was going to kill him if they didn't believe him. Sure, he put on that act of being all tough and cool and not giving a shit about anything, but she'd seen inside him. Now she knew more about it and about him, she knew this was going to devastate him.

Surely his parents would believe him. They loved him; they had to. He was their son. Yeah, they'd had some problems. Tyler hadn't made his teenage years easy, she'd admit that, but even so, didn't parents love their children unconditionally? She knew hers had. And apparently Nick's.

She strained her ears to hear what was being said.

"Why the hell would you wait..." she heard Dr. Wirth say.

She chewed on her bottom lip and looked at Nick.

She could tell them.

There wasn't much else she could do to make this right, but Dr. and Mrs. Wirth liked her and respected her and if she told them the truth, they'd probably believe her. She covered her eyes. Telling them she was there that night ten years ago wasn't that bad. So she'd walked in on something she shouldn't have. That bad burning feeling inside her intensified and sweat popped out on her forehead. She'd have to admit she'd stood there and watched. To Tyler. And to his parents.

She swiped her forehead and leaned her elbows on the counter. Her hair fell forward as she bent her head. Nick's hand landed on her back and rubbed in slow, warm circles. "Hey," he whispered. She didn't move.

But worse than that was admitting *she* was the girl they'd taken up to their hotel room Friday night. A wave of seasick panic washed over her and she gasped for air.

Oh for— It wasn't that bad. So she went up to their room. After she'd kissed both of them. She could have gone up there for one drink and left. They didn't have to know all the details.

Except...she could tell them she knew Tyler and Nick would never do that to a woman, because of how they'd treated her.

Her stomach turned over again and she fought to get oxygen into her lungs.

What was really important here? So what if Dr. and Mrs. Wirth thought she was a tramp? So what if they told the whole town? Did that really matter when Tyler was being crushed by his parents, the parents he'd always wanted love and respect from, the parents who'd never given it to him even though she knew now he deserved it. He always had. Maybe he'd gotten in a few scrapes, but it's not as if he did drugs or stole cars or joined a gang and killed people, for god's sake.

If she'd learned nothing else from the tragedy that had happened to her father, it was that she shouldn't worry about what people thought of them. Her dad couldn't help the way he was. He'd still been a good person. And so was she.

She sucked in a big breath, straightened and turned to Nick. "I have to do something."

Chapter Thirteen

Tyler sat on the chair in the den. Tiger Woods was teeing off silently on the television, the sound muted. His parents kept asking him questions that seemed as if they were basically calling him a liar and a depraved pervert. He tried to tell himself it didn't matter.

He tried to tell himself he didn't feel anything, not the burning in his stomach, the stabbing feeling in his chest, the pounding in his head. It didn't matter.

"Why the hell would you wait this long to try to tell us that?" his father demanded. "Don't you think it would have carried a lot more weight ten years ago? When it happened?"

"Would it?" Tyler slouched in the chair. "Would it have carried more weight? You were always ready to believe the worst of me." He shrugged. "It was just easier to let you."

"Ken." Mom shot a glare at his dad. "He's talking to us. Would you just listen, for once?"

Tyler blinked at her. *Whoa, Mom.*

"If you're trying to tell us nothing happened the other night," Dad said harshly, apparently ignoring her. "Forget it! Why would Les Pearson make that up?"

"Who the hell is Les Pearson?" Tyler asked.

"He works at the front desk of the hotel," Mom said,

shooting Dad another glance loaded with annoyance. "He's the one who saw you. He saw you. You and Nick both..." She stopped.

"I'm not trying to tell you nothing happened that night," Tyler said. "I'm trying to tell you that what did happen was completely consensual, all of us adults, and frankly, none of your business."

"He's right."

Tyler's head snapped around and he looked at Kaelin standing in the door. His jaw went slack. His parents, too, gaped at her.

"Kaelin, dear. What are you doing here? Were we..." Mom looked like she was in agony. "Were we making too much noise?" The idea that the family was making a scene was clearly horrifying to her. God forbid someone might hear their family argument. Another set of French doors, closed, led to the living room where Avery and Scott hosted a few friends and relatives.

"No," Kaelin said. "You weren't."

He looked at her standing there, slender, dressed in her usual knee-length skirt, today white cotton, with a flowery top. Her brown hair hung in soft waves over her shoulders and her full bottom lip trembled ever so slightly. Her fingers were curled into her palms.

"I know what you're talking about," Kaelin said, advancing into the den. She pressed her lips together briefly. "And I want you to know the truth."

She knew...wait. What?

Nick followed behind her, and Tyler's eyes shot to Nick's face. Tyler's eyebrows lifted in a question. He jumped to his feet. "Did you tell her?"

Nick nodded somberly.

"Jesus fucking Christ." Tyler lifted a hand to his forehead and turned away. He'd never wanted Kaelin to know about that. Never, ever. Had sworn his family, Nick and especially Avery to secrecy, to never tell her what he'd been accused of doing that night. He did not want her to know. His throat tightened. Shit.

He looked at Kaelin, expecting to see hatred and anger and who knew what else.

Instead he saw warmth and love and concern. His chest constricted.

She turned to his parents. "There are some things you need to know," she said quietly. "That night ten years ago—I was there."

Mom gasped. Dad's mouth fell open.

"I wasn't supposed to be," she said. "They didn't know I was coming over." Tyler's heart tightened even more and he clenched his hands into fists and closed his eyes. "When I saw Tyler and Nick and Tracy, I was shocked." She didn't look at him. "But I...I was..." She bent her head, her hair obscuring her face. She was what?

"I watched them," she said, so quietly Tyler could barely hear. "For about ten minutes."

Tyler had to sit down. His legs pretty much gave out on him, and he collapsed onto the chair he'd been sitting in. He stared at Kaelin. What was she saying? Did she know who she was saying this to? If this had been any other time, he'd wonder if she was drunk. But no. She was not drunk.

She'd watched them for ten minutes?

Oh Christ. He covered his eyes with his hand. He never knew that. Oh Christ.

"Tracy was definitely there of her own free will, Mrs. Wirth," she continued. "I can attest to that. She wanted everything that was happening. She was begging for it."

Mom's mouth opened and closed like a fish, her eyes buggy, her face scarlet. His dad didn't look much different, running a finger around the inside of the collar of his Ralph Lauren polo shirt.

"I interrupted them," Kaelin said. "They were all shocked to see me there, including Tracy. I ran out as soon as they saw me, but Nick told me nothing more happened after that. Tracy changed her mind and they took her home. And I believe them."

"You don't know for sure nothing happened after that," Dad snapped. "She said—"

"You'd rather believe a stranger over your son?" Kaelin asked slowly, her eyebrows drawn down. "Really? Because I believe Tyler and Nick. I believe them because..." She drew in another long breath. "Because it was me at the hotel with them Friday night."

Jesus Christ. All Tyler could think was a string of shocking curse words. What the fuck was she doing?

His mom was choking. Was she having a heart attack?

His dad reached for her and drew her down to the couch beside him. "Are you okay, Margot?" he asked.

She shoved his hands away with a glare. "Yes. I mean, no. I mean...Kaelin, dear..."

"Kaelin." Tyler spoke up. "Stop this. Now."

She faced him. "No. I'm not stopping. I want them to know the truth. About you."

"But what about you, for Chrissake?"

"I don't care about me. I don't care if they know the truth about me. I am who I am." She held his gaze steadily.

Now *he* was the one having a heart attack, the pain in his chest so severe it took his breath away. She had no fucking intention of leaving this damn town and she was standing there trashing her reputation in front of the two people to whom reputation meant the most. Meant more, apparently, than he did.

"I was with them Friday night. That whole thing was my idea. I was the one who wanted to do it. Don't blame Tyler. And...I can assure you that based on my experience, there is no way either of those men would ever force a woman to have sex." Her voice started quavering despite the way her jaw was lifted. "I won't be so crass as to share details with you, as I'm sure you don't want to hear it, but I want you to know that."

Tyler looked at his mom, who sat there with her hand pressed to her heart, and strangely, a faint smile on her lips.

"Since we're confessing..." They all swiveled to look at Avery in the now open French doors to the living room. Her flushed cheeks indicated she'd been listening to them. She took another step into the room, and Scott followed her and closed the door behind him, a worried expression creasing his high forehead. "You might as well also know that it wasn't Tyler who wrote off the car that first summer I was home from college. It was me."

"Avery!"

So many people in the room gasped her name it was like a chorus. Tyler covered his eyes with one hand. *What the fuck now?*

"I'd been drinking," she continued. "He took the rap for me because he was sober. And because he's my brother..." Her voice cracked. "And he loved me. And it always killed me that he never bothered to tell you the truth about so many things, just let you assume the worst. And then you kicked him out and..." A sob escaped her. Scott wrapped his arms around her and hugged her.

Tyler leaned his head back and looked at the ceiling.

"I tried so hard," Avery sobbed. "I tried so hard to be perfect so everyone would be happy, and it never worked. It only made things worse."

Silence filled the room, other than a few small sniffles from Avery against Scott's chest. Tyler's lungs burned as he filled them with air, straightened his shoulders and looked at everyone.

"You are all fucking nuts," he snarled. "Avery, why the hell did you do that?"

"It doesn't matter anymore!" she cried. "The truth matters! I can't stand it anymore. I wanted you home for my wedding. I wanted us to be a family and there was all this tension and I hate it!"

"Oh, Avery," Mom whispered, her hands to her mouth.

He groaned. Then looked at Kaelin. She watched him, eyes still full of concern and a kind of wariness. "Kaelin."

She lowered her chin and looked at him through her long eyelashes, her pretty mouth tight.

"You shouldn't have done that," he said to her through clenched teeth. "Are you crazy?"

"I did it for you," she whispered. "Tyler..."

Oh hell. There they went again. Like that summer, that hot, aching, wonderful summer, she'd started to get all gooey over him when he didn't deserve it. Not from her. "Don't! You shouldn't have done it for me!" he shouted, aware that everyone in the room was staring. "I'm not worth it! And you were wrong about one thing. One little detail."

She blinked at him, eyes glossy, fingers trembling.

"That night you walked in on us...I *did* know you were coming. I heard you talking to Avery about coming to get some books from her room. I knew you were coming and I planned

177

that little scene and timed it perfectly so you'd walk in on it."

Her gasp felt like a blade in his chest. Pain ripped through him but he kept going. "I wanted you to see it. I wanted you to know what an asshole I was. How sick and depraved Nick and I both were. You needed to know the truth, and I did that on fucking purpose."

Kaelin put out a hand as if trying to find something to hold on to, but there was nothing near her and she stumbled and almost fell. Nick took two steps and grabbed her, held her up, his arms wrapped around her. Tyler wanted to put his fist through the wall, kick down the goddamn perfect French doors. His jaw was so tight his teeth hurt, his belly muscles rigid, his short fingernails biting into his palms.

"Jesus, Tyler," Nick said to him. As usual the one who had to step in and try to make his fuck-up right. "Jesus."

"Let's go," Tyler snarled. He strode toward the door, right past Kaelin and Nick, didn't look at Avery and Scott or his parents. "I gotta get out of here."

He stood in the kitchen for a moment, fighting for breath, hands clenched, waiting for Nick. Who came moments later.

Nick shook his head and looked at him. "Christ, Tyler. You make it so *fucking* hard to love you."

Tyler stopped short, turned to Nick and stared him down, then shot a glance back into the other room. "Then don't," he growled at him. "Just fucking don't love me. I'm an asshole."

Chapter Fourteen

Kaelin watched Tyler leave, the room shifting around her. Her ears buzzed, her heart hurt. She put a hand to her chest and closed her eyes. She didn't know who she hurt for more—him or herself.

He'd done that deliberately, that night, just so she would see them? Just so she would be hurt and leave him alone?

The thought ripped a hole in her gut, just tore her apart. She'd known he didn't have the same feelings for her as she was developing for him, and she'd thought she hadn't really shown those feelings. But apparently she had and he'd been...whatever. All she knew was, he wanted to get rid of her.

Had she trailed after him and Nick all summer like a lovesick puppy? Surely to god not. Humiliation burned a hole inside her. That he'd gone to that length to hurt her...oh lord. She pressed a hand to her stomach, opened her eyes and met Avery's anguished and questioning gaze.

"Kaelin. Come on." Avery detached herself from her new husband's embrace, grabbed Kaelin's hand and dragged her out of the room, up the stairs and into the bedroom where they'd stood yesterday, Avery in her beautiful wedding dress looking so shiny and happy, now all tear-streaked and anguished.

"Sit." Avery pushed her to the bed. Kaelin lowered herself on shaky legs and stared at the rug on the floor.

"You were with Tyler and Nick Friday night?"

She lifted heavy eyes to look at Avery. The time for lies and secrets was over, apparently. Even Avery had confessed. "Yes," she said. She lifted her chin, ready for Avery's censure, her disapproval. But Avery just looked puzzled. "I was. It just happened. We'd gotten Scott and Hardeep back to their rooms. They were walking out with me and we stopped to sit in the lobby for a few minutes. We were talking and then I just...it was me." She gave a short nod of her head. "It was me who instigated it, so don't think badly of Tyler."

"I...okay."

"They kept saying how nice I was. And I was just sick of being nice and good and...boring. So I kissed them both. Things got carried away." She closed her eyes, remembering just how far. Some things were going to be left to Avery's imagination. "I spent all night with them."

"Oh my god," Avery breathed, fingertips on her lips, staring at Kaelin. "You wild woman, you."

"I'm sorry."

"Don't apologize!"

"But he's your brother. Your younger brother." She took a deep breath, ready to tell the rest. "I never told you about that summer. That summer we were talking about when I caught Nick and Tyler with Tracy."

Avery pressed her lips together. "No."

"Did you know about that? What she accused them of?"

"Yes. I knew it couldn't be true. I knew my parents kicked him out." Her voice wobbled. "And I knew he begged me never to tell you about it, because he didn't want you to know."

"I don't understand that. And god, I wish you'd told me! I could have set your parents straight about that ten years ago, and maybe avoided that whole big mess."

Avery bit down on her bottom lip. "Oh geez."

"And why didn't he want you to tell me? I don't get it."

"Kaelin, don't you see?"

Kaelin shook her head, moisture gathering in the corners of her eyes. Her throat tightened up.

"He cared about you. I think he still does."

Kaelin choked. "Yeah right! Cared enough about me to set that whole thing up so I'd see it and he didn't have to tell me to get lost." She bent her head. "I never realized he knew how I felt."

"Why didn't you tell me about it? About you and him."

Kaelin didn't look up, just stared down at her fingers clasped on her lap. "That was the summer you were dating Thomas Alsworth. You were crazy about him. You spent all your time with him and his friends."

She heard Avery's softly indrawn breath.

"It was okay," she said, reaching for Avery's hand. "I was happy for you. I just felt a little at loose ends. Home from college. I was working and looking after my dad, but we had that caregiver coming in sometimes and I had evenings and weekends with no studying. For some reason I ended up hanging around with Tyler and Nick. I'm not sure how it happened, mostly by accident, but they started including me in their plans. We went to the beach." She paused. "We went to bush parties and drank beer and danced in the grass and skinny-dipped. I was doing things I'd never done before. It felt wild. Exciting. I thought they wanted me with them. I thought they were having fun too. And I also didn't tell you because I didn't think you'd be very happy about me...er...being with your little brother. He was two years younger than us."

Avery released her hand and edged closer, slid her arm around Kaelin's shoulders.

"One night Tyler and I were alone for a while and...he kissed me."

That kiss, although not her first, had been the hottest, most intensely erotic kiss of her life. Until this weekend. She'd been burning up, melting down, on fire for him.

"I was so silly. He was so cool and popular. So many girls were after him. And I thought that was maybe the start of...something. But then the next night I came here to get those books from your room and...well, you know now what I found."

"I'm sorry."

"It's not your fault."

"I know, but I'm sorry that happened to you."

"I knew he could be a little mean, like, teasing mean. He made fun of me all the time, you know? But to deliberately hurt me like that." She shook her head.

"You heard why he did it."

"Yeah. To get rid of me."

Avery shifted on the bed, and turned Kaelin by her shoulders to face to her. "That's not exactly what he said. He said it was because he didn't think he was good enough for you."

"He never said that." Had he? It was all kind of fuzzy and mixed up.

"He said he's not worth it. You know what he's like."

Kaelin gazed at her friend in puzzlement, thinking back. "He said that's why I shouldn't have told his parents about it. Oh, I don't understand him! He's so damn complicated!"

She pressed her hands to her burning eyes.

"Yes, he is," Avery agreed. "But I love him. I would so like him to be happy."

"He and Nick..." She shot a sideways glance at Avery.

"Are they together?" Avery asked in a low voice.

"Sort of. I think you need to hear about that from him."

"'Sort of.' Another complication. It figures." She shook her head. "But I really think he has feelings for you, Kaelin."

Kaelin's head throbbed. "I need to go home. I need to think about this. I'm not sure what I've done. I may have just done myself out of a job. If word about all this gets out..."

"My parents aren't ones to spread gossip," Avery said quietly. "You know what they're like. They're not going to want anyone to know about this, any more than you do."

"Well, they may not, but I don't think the guy working the front desk at the hotel has any compunction about gossiping apparently. And if Brent hears about that..."

"Brent?" Avery frowned. "I thought you weren't seeing him anymore."

"I'm not." She told Avery about him pulling her over the morning before, and how he'd seen her and jumped to the conclusion—accurately—that she hadn't been home that night.

"Oh. Well." Avery nibbled a fingernail.

"You know what? Truthfully? I don't care. I don't care anymore. It doesn't matter."

"Remember you could still come to Los Angeles."

"Yeah." Kaelin nodded. Leaving Mapleglen was becoming more appealing.

"Or you could go to Chicago."

Her eyes flew open and her gaze clashed with Avery's. "Chicago?"

Avery nodded, watching her.

"Why would I go there? Tyler and Nick don't want me. Didn't you hear him? He was so pissed off at me, now, and ten years ago when I cramped his style..."

"Was he pissed off at you Friday night?"

Kaelin shifted back. "Um...no."

"Was he pissed off at you Saturday? After?"

Kaelin shook her head. "Not until I followed him up to the hotel room after your mom asked him to leave the wedding."

"Why was he angry then?"

"I don't know! Maybe he was just taking his anger at your mom out on me! But it seemed like he was pissed off because I'd come up to their room with them, again."

"I see." Avery tapped her bottom lip with one finger. "He was probably worried about you and your reputation again."

Kaelin tipped her head to one side. "I suppose."

"Think about it," Avery said. "Think about him and think about going to Chicago." She rose to her feet and moved to the dresser. She poked around in some things she'd left there yesterday then held up a small card in two fingers. "You don't have to move there. I know that's a big step. But you're on vacation for the next two weeks. Why not go visit and see him and talk about stuff and see what happens? I really think he does care, Kaelin. Yeah, he was angry, but I think you can figure out why." She walked over and handed Kaelin the card. It was Tyler's business card, with his home address written on the back.

Kaelin's eyes teared up again and she swiped at them. "I don't know if I can figure him out. I don't know if I *want* to figure him out. Oh god, I don't know what I want." She stood too. "I'm sorry, Ave. This is your wedding weekend and everything got so messed up."

"Not because of you. My family had all this shit we needed to get out in the open. Who knows, maybe things will be better after this."

"Things won't be better if they don't look at Tyler and see who he really is."

"Who is he, really?" Avery's voice was gentle.

"He's strong and smart and charming and energetic. He'd do anything for people he loves. He's determined." Avery's eyes grew warm as she watched Kaelin and listened to her. "He put himself through college after your parents threw him out."

"You know, he never came right out and told me that, but I knew things were tough for him financially. Shit."

"And look where he is now."

Avery nodded, and smiled knowingly. "Yeah."

"Anyway. If your parents value their reputation and image more than they value him, well, it's their loss. But I don't think you can expect him to start coming to a lot of family reunions."

Avery nodded, her mouth turning down at the corners. "Yeah. You're right."

"I'm going home now," Kaelin said.

"Thank you again for all you did." She caught her bottom lip between her teeth. "My mom would have had things so over the top. I couldn't handle getting sucked into that old pattern, of her taking over and telling me what to do. I wanted it to be my wedding, and I was afraid I wasn't strong enough to stand up to her."

Kaelin bent her head. And Avery thought *she* was? "Oh, Avery. Of course you are."

Avery shook her head. "I know it was a lot of work to deal with her, but she loves you."

Kaelin snorted. "Probably not anymore." They hugged tightly.

The long drive back to Chicago was mostly silent. Nick flipped through copies of trade magazines as Tyler drove. His jaw ached, his neck and shoulders so tight every movement was painful.

He thought. A lot. About all kinds of things. About his parents. About the glum realization of how much he'd contributed to the discord between them. How stubborn and stupid he'd been.

He thought about Avery and her confession, a sad admiration filling him at her courage. Of course, years later, there wasn't much that was going to happen. His parents would still love her. Nobody was going to throw her in jail over that now. But she'd done it for him and she hadn't had to, and that filled him with a funny warm glow.

But mostly he thought about Kaelin and how crazy brave she'd been to walk in there and spill her guts. God. And he thought about the hurt look on her face when he'd yelled at her, and especially when he told her he'd deliberately set up that scene so she'd see it. She'd looked ready to fall on the floor.

Shit.

"Gotta stop for gas," he said to Nick. Nick just grunted.

He pulled off the interstate when he saw the sign for a service station, stood there filling the Jeep as sunshine warmed his face and the June breeze ran soft fingers through his hair. Nick got out and used the bathroom and he did too after he paid for the gas, then they climbed back in and resumed their drive home without saying more than a few words.

And he had to think about Nick too. Nick sitting there beside him, quiet, unreadable. Was he pissed at him? Disappointed in him? Feeling sorry for him? He thought about Nick's comment earlier, about how insulting it was to him that Tyler thought Kaelin was too good for him—but Nick wasn't. The guy drove him crazy, had pushed him into doing that, and look what a mess it had turned out to be. Yet he couldn't blame him and he knew Nick was right. He had to get this chip off his shoulder and move on.

He'd actually thought he had, over the years, that it had just faded away, until he'd gone home and all those old emotions had resurrected it, a big hulking chip monster sitting on his shoulder, making him say and do things he knew were so fucked up.

Nick was right. It was time to grow up. He'd tried to tell his parents. It hadn't worked. Oh well. At least he'd done it. He'd come clean with everyone. He'd hurt Kaelin, but once again, that was for the best. Sleeping with her hadn't been the smartest thing he'd ever done. But it had been the hottest. And the most incredibly emotional and moving and...forget it.

Maybe after his parents thought about it, they'd realize he was telling the truth. Or maybe not. But at least he'd done it, and whatever the outcome was, he'd deal with it. Having the respect and love of his parents would be nice, but he could live without it and at least he now had the satisfaction and self-respect of knowing he'd made an effort and tried to set things right.

The only thing that worried him was what the fallout was going to be from Kaelin's impetuous confession. If word got out about her, she was going to find life in Mapleglen difficult. He gnawed on the inside of his cheek as he drove and thought about that. About what he could do about that.

Not much.

Dammit. Why the *fuck* had she done that? Pressure built inside him again, thinking about it, wishing she was there so he could turn her over his knee and spank her cute little ass. Gah.

Once they were home and in their apartment, Nick opened the refrigerator and stared into it. "Got nothing to eat," he said.

"Order pizza," Tyler said, heading into his bedroom to change. He tossed jeans and T-shirt into the hamper and found a pair of baggy shorts and a clean shirt. When he returned to the living room, Nick had changed too, into similar clothes.

"Pizza'll be here in forty minutes," he said. He threw himself onto the couch. "You ready to talk yet? I thought your head was gonna explode on the way home, you were thinking so hard."

Tyler smiled reluctantly and sat beside Nick. "I don't want to talk."

"I know."

Tyler eyed his buddy. "I did what you wanted me to."

"Yeah." Nick nodded. "You faced your parents, told them the truth."

"I don't think they believed me."

Nick held his gaze. "You can't control that. But at least you manned up and did your part."

"Yeah."

After a pause, Nick said, "What about Kaelin?"

"What about her?"

"You were pretty hard on her."

"I was pissed at her! Why'd she do that, the stupid little idiot!"

"She's not stupid. And you know why she did it."

Tyler blew out a breath. "Yeah, I know, and like I said,

she's a stupid idiot to even think of doing something like that for me."

Nick sighed.

Kaelin sat on the small deck off the back of her house on Monday, the house she'd grown up in, the house her parents had left her after they'd both died. She could have sold it, bought herself something that was her own, and in fact she wasn't sure why she hadn't. It was an older house and there were always things that needed fixing that she didn't know how to do. Money had been tight with her dad not working and she'd had to do a lot of fixing up over the last few years.

Yeah, there were happy memories there, but there were some tough ones, too, the despair and frustration of realizing her dad was never going to be the same, the embarrassment of him acting like a child sometimes, so difficult to handle for a teenager who didn't like to attract attention to herself. Eventually she'd come to terms with it, realized she still loved her dad because he was her dad, even though he was really a different person, and no longer felt embarrassed but just accepted him for who he was.

She'd have the memories of her happy childhood no matter where she lived, so that wasn't the reason she didn't sell the house and move. She knew it was just because she was safe and secure there, with a roof over her head that was paid for, and that selling the house and finding a new place was scary.

Taz leaped off the deck and tore after a squirrel who'd dared to enter his yard, his sharp little bark deceptively ferocious. He stood at the foot of the maple tree, barking so hard all four feet lifted off the ground. She smiled. "C'mere, Taz," she called. "Come."

Taz turned and trotted back to her, leaped lightly onto her lap and put his little front feet on her chest to try to kiss her. She turned her head and let him lick her chin, then picked him up and hugged his solid, furry little body. She closed her eyes then set Taz on the deck.

She picked up her glass of iced tea and sipped it. The grass needed cutting. One more thing that needed to be done. Sometimes she paid Dillon down the street to cut it for her. Maybe she should go see if he was home. Summer vacation and its long empty days had kids his age, too young for a job but old enough to want to make a little money, looking for things like that to do.

Maybe in a while. She still felt tired, so tired, after that crazy weekend. Much of it was emotional exhaustion, she knew. She hadn't taken Avery's advice yet, hadn't let herself think about Tyler because...she was afraid.

Shaking her head, she rose to her feet. Never mind finding Dillon, she'd cut the grass herself. She needed to keep busy, her two weeks of vacation stretching out empty in front of her giving her a hollow aching feeling inside. Actually her whole life stretched out empty in front of her. And the hollow ache intensified. But as she stepped off the deck, Margot Wirth appeared at her gate.

"Hi, Kaelin."

Kaelin's feet halted in surprise. "Hi, Mrs. Wirth. How are you? Is there something you need?" She thought about wedding decorations and flowers and gifts...was there something she'd forgotten to do?

"No. Just to talk to you for a few minutes. If that's okay."

Kaelin studied Mrs. Wirth's face, the tension in her mouth and at the corners of her eyes, the shadows beneath her eyes. "Of course." This had to be about yesterday. Geez. Mrs. Wirth was probably angry at her for her part in that big scene. Great. "Can I get you something to drink? Lemonade? Coffee?"

"No thanks. I'm fine."

"Let's sit." Kaelin indicated the wicker chairs on her deck.

Mrs. Wirth took a seat, setting her designer handbag on the deck. She clasped her fingers together in her lap. "How are you, dear? Are you okay?"

"I'm fine." Kaelin hesitated. "How are you?" She regarded her friend's mother with a touch of worry. Yesterday probably hadn't been a real fun day at the Wirth home.

"I'm okay." She gave a small smile. "I'm sorry that you got dragged into our family mess yesterday."

Kaelin blinked. "Well. I sort of contributed to it."

Mrs. Wirth's smile went crooked. "You were very brave yesterday."

Now Kaelin's mouth fell open. "Um. Brave?"

"What you did was very...noble. For Tyler."

"I just thought everyone should know the truth."

"Yes. The truth is important." She hesitated. "I want to tell you something. About me."

"Okay." Kaelin eyed her.

"When I was twenty, I got pregnant. With Avery. It was an accident. I was in college. Ken was much older and he insisted we get married. He wanted me to drop out of college and stay home with the baby. I was young, and in some ways, it was nice to have someone look after me, and Avery. Ken was a doctor and he made good money and I thought it would be a good life, married to him."

Kaelin processed all this, a little mystified, not sure what to say.

"And it has been a good life. I love my husband and I love my children. Once Avery was born, I just wanted to be the best mother I could be. But it wasn't what I pictured my life to be, when I was a twenty-year-old college student. And despite everything I've had, I've often felt a little...empty. As if I wanted more, which I told myself was just selfish and greedy. Considering how much I had." Again she paused, then met Kaelin's eyes. "I see some of that in you."

Kaelin sat back in her chair, dropping her gaze to her knees. "Oh. Well."

"You don't have to tell me about it," Mrs. Wirth said quickly. "I know you've had to give up things in your life. I also know you're happy here, in some ways. But, Kaelin, dear, if there are things in life that you want, you should go after them. Now. Before you're fifty years old and wondering what you've done with your life."

Like her? Kaelin's head spun, her image of Mrs. Wirth being turned inside out. She'd always been so perfect, the perfect wife, the perfect mother, with the perfect home. The idea that Mrs. Wirth felt this way boggled the mind.

"I'm not sure what you mean," she said, in a near-whisper.

"Yes you are." Mrs. Wirth gazed at her shrewdly.

Kaelin wanted to squirm in her chair. Mrs. Wirth knew a lot about her, after the last couple of days. Things she never would have dreamed of telling her. And yet, still she looked at her with affection and understanding. Kaelin's throat tightened.

"I can't...I'm afraid," she choked out.

"What are you afraid of?"

"I'm afraid because I want things I can't have. And I'm afraid I want things I *can* have. And that scares me even more."

"I don't think you need to be as afraid as you are," Mrs.

Wirth said. "Are you worried about your job?"

"Yes." She bit her lip. "If this gets out..."

"People love you, Kaelin. You might be surprised." She rose to her feet. "I have to go." She opened her arms for a hug and Kaelin too rose from her chair and went into her arms. "Think about what I said, okay?" She drew back and smiled at Kaelin.

"Yes. I will."

Mrs. Wirth picked up her purse and left, and for some reason Kaelin felt like Mrs. Wirth was saying goodbye for a long time. Weird.

In a daze, she headed toward the garage where she kept her lawnmower. Cutting the grass didn't stop her brain from working, though, as she pushed the mower back and forth over the small lawn first out front then in back. She kept hearing Mrs. Wirth's words about going after what she wanted, and Nick's words about whether she'd find that "something wilder" she wanted in Mapleglen and Avery's words about Tyler caring about her. Avery had told her to think about why he'd been so angry at her. Yesterday. Saturday night. Ten years ago.

Could Avery be right? Could it be because he cared? But if he cared about her, why? Why would he push her away like that? Did Mrs. Wirth think the same thing?

She remembered pieces of their conversation that night in the hotel room, about how he never could live up to his parents' expectations so he'd given up trying. About how it was easier to just let them think the worst of him. How she'd accused him of mocking her to make up for his own insecurities.

Her feet slowed and stopped in the middle of the yard as she stared at the big maple tree in the corner. Did he really think so little of himself that he thought he didn't deserve to be loved? Had his parents really done that much of a number on him?

And yet he'd made such a life for himself—put himself through college, begun a successful career in a tough industry in a big city. She'd seen his accomplishments in those secret internet searches—the awards he'd won, the big advertising campaigns he'd been a part of, magazine articles about him even.

He'd been angry the night of the wedding after his parents had asked him to leave, and yeah, maybe some of that had been misplaced and directed at her when she'd come after him along with Nick. But maybe he really had been angry because she was putting her reputation at risk by doing that.

Her reputation. She rolled her eyes then realized she was still standing in the middle of the yard and pushed forward again. What exactly was a reputation anyway? Mrs. Wirth had said that people loved her. People who cared about her knew her and knew if she was a good or a bad person. People had judged her dad after his injury, because he was different, but he wasn't a bad person because of it.

She wasn't going to run away from Mapleglen because of that. If they fired her over some rumors that nobody could prove, she'd sue them for wrongful dismissal. If people didn't want to talk to her or didn't want her to visit them at the seniors' home, that was their problem. She'd lived through people looking at them and talking about them and feeling sorry for them once before when her dad had been hurt, and she could do it again.

If she left Mapleglen it wasn't going to be because of that. It wasn't going to be because she was running away in fear. It was going to be because she was brave enough to start over.

She felt a compelling need to see Tyler again. And Nick. To reassure them of that. So they knew that even though she'd done what she had, to her it didn't really seem like any kind of sacrifice. She wanted Tyler's parents to know the truth and so she'd told it.

There was no reason she couldn't go to Chicago for a few days.

Other than Taz. She gazed at her little dog and bit her lip. What would she do with him? She couldn't put him in a kennel. She just couldn't. Maybe one of the neighbors...

"Hi, Kaelin."

She looked up to see Dillon standing at her gate. "Hey, Dillon. How are you?"

Taz ran to the boy, tail wagging, yipping excitedly. Dillon grinned and held out a hand to Taz to sniff, then bent and picked him up. "I came to see if you wanted your lawn mowed, but I guess I'm too late."

She smiled back at him. "Yeah. I'm just about finished for today. But how would you feel about dog sitting? And maybe a regular job cutting the grass for the next while. I'm thinking of going on a little trip."

Chapter Fifteen

Friday night Tyler walked into the apartment. He'd done the happy hour networking thing after work for a couple of hours while Nick—the numbers guy, not the people guy like Tyler was—went to the gym to work out. Nick still wasn't home, the apartment was empty. Tyler yanked at the tie around his neck, but stopped at the fridge for another beer before changing.

What a fucking brutal week. He and Nick were still at odds over the Healthy Solutions contract and they had to make a decision by Monday one way or the other. They'd dicked around long enough. Other problems had come up and Tyler knew he wasn't able to deal with them with his usual quick decisiveness. He was distracted and restless and grouchy. His neck and shoulders were killing him. He was going to have to make an appointment to see his massage therapist. Nick hadn't been offering to do the massage he often did. And that was another thing that was fucking with Tyler's head. He hated that things between him and Nick were strained.

He guzzled down some of the beer, flipped through the mail. Bills. Crap. He tossed them onto the desk. He rubbed the back of his neck. He'd thought once he'd had it out with his parents things were supposed to be better. Ha.

A knock at the door startled him. What...? Did Nick forget

his keys or something?

He strode to the door and flung it open.

Kaelin stood there.

He stared at her. She gazed back at him.

"What are you doing here?" he asked.

"Nice greeting." She stood there in a pretty pink flowered sundress and flip-flops, her purse slung over her shoulder. "I was in the neighborhood and thought I'd stop by."

He regarded her dumbly. "You were?"

She bit her lip, starting to look a little uncertain. Then he noticed that her fingers on the strap of her purse were shaking. Just a little. "No," she whispered.

"Come in." He stood aside to let her into the apartment.

She walked in and looked around. "Nice place," she said, standing in the middle of the living room. The older building had been recently renovated, the oak hardwood floors refinished, the original creamy brick walls cleaned and new windows installed in the arched frames looking out onto the tree-lined street.

"Thanks. It's a lot better than the dump we lived in during college. How'd you know where we live?"

"Avery gave me your address."

"Ah."

She turned to face him, looking so pretty and fragile, her slender calves bare beneath the hem of the dress, curvy arms revealed by the narrow straps. Her breasts rose and fell as she breathed in shallow breaths. Her eyes flickered. Again, they both just stared at each other in thick, sticky silence.

"Uh, want a beer?"

"Sure."

Her answer surprised him. She didn't seem like a beer-drinking kind of girl. When he said so, walking to the small galley kitchen, she replied, "Beer reminds me of that summer we were hanging out."

Hanging out. Yeah. They'd been hanging out. Having fun. Falling in love.

Christ. He closed his eyes, one hand on the handle of the fridge door, then yanked it open and pulled out another beer.

"Nick's not home?" she asked.

He found a glass and handed her the beer and the glass. "No. He's at the gym."

"Oh. Yeah, I could tell he's been working out a lot."

"He should be home soon. Ah, have a seat." He gestured to the big leather sectional.

She perched on the edge of the couch, her purse on the floor, her beer clasped in both hands. Awareness sparked between them. He wanted to grab her and pull her onto his lap and kiss the breath out of her.

"So. You gonna tell me why you're really here?"

"Okay. I just wanted you to know that..." Her voice went low and throaty. "I just wanted you to know that you didn't have to be mad at me for telling your parents the truth. Even if you were just mad because..." She stopped and swallowed. "Because you were worried about me, you don't have to be. Because I'm fine. And I wanted you to know that. To know that I'd already been thinking about leaving Mapleglen, and if I do, someday, it won't be because of that. It'll be because I want to."

He watched her, listened to her, his gut tight, her bravery and courage making his heart turn over in his chest and ache. Christ, she was special.

He rubbed the back of his neck. "I'm sorry, Kaelin."

She regarded him warily. "Sorry for what?"

He sighed, bent his head, the words stuck in his throat. "I'm sorry for what I did. I'm sorry for what I said. I'm sorry I keep acting like an asshole, especially to you."

Waves of silence had him lifting his head to peer at her. Her face shone with trails of silvery tears, her bottom lip full and quivery.

"Fuck!" He slammed his beer onto the coffee table and shifted across the couch toward her. "Don't cry! Jesus, I did it again!" She came into his arms willingly, her body slender and trembling against his. He pressed her wet face to his shoulder. "I'm sorry, sweet baby, I'm so sorry."

"Why did you do it?" she asked, her voice muffled in his dress shirt. "Why did you want to hurt me that way? That night..."

"You mean with Tracy?"

"Yes."

"I didn't want to hurt you. I just wanted you to know the truth about me."

"What truth? That you like to tie girls up?"

"Yeah. That. But mostly just that I was no good for you."

"Oh, Tyler." She sighed. "If you weren't interested, you should have just told me that."

He snorted. "No shit. Would've saved myself and Nick a whole helluva lot of grief if we hadn't done that, that night. How was I supposed to know Tracy was going to freak out like that? Telling you would have been the smart thing to do, but I never claimed to be that smart. And besides, I *was* interested in you."

She lifted her head and gazed at him with big, wet, questioning eyes. He eased a strand of hair off her face. "But I was still no good for you," he said. "I was in trouble more often than not. I did like to tie up girls. I did like to screw around with Nick. I was so messed up."

She closed her eyes and looked as if someone was breaking her fingers. "You're such an idiot, Tyler."

"I know. I fucked up a lot of things. Believe me, I know."

He brushed a kiss over her mouth, that soft, sweet mouth. Her lips parted. Their eyes met. Their breath mingled. His eyes closed as he moved in for another kiss, long, slow and warm. One hand slid over her hip, rested on her waist, the other smoothed over her jaw, rubbing away the tears. A wave of such intense pleasure and heat washed over him, he groaned into her mouth.

He deepened the kiss, slid his hand into her silky hair and cupped the back of her head, his tongue sliding inside her mouth in slow strokes, tasting her. She tasted sweet, so sweet, the sweetest girl he'd ever known, but he also knew she was more than just sweet, she was as dark and deep as he was. It was the difference between vanilla soft-serve and the extra dark Scharffen Berger chocolate he loved.

She kissed him back, her mouth opening to him, her tongue rubbing on his, making small moaning noises in her throat, trembling in his arms. She pressed her whole body into him, especially soft breasts against his chest. She wrapped her arms around his head and held on, and they kissed, endless, long, drugging tongue kisses.

"Kaelin," he whispered, his cheek pressed to hers. "Christ, Kaelin. You scare the crap out of me."

He felt her smile and she rubbed her face against his beard stubble. "The big bad boy is scared," she murmured, fingers drifting across his shoulders, into his hair, sending pleasure cascading down his body.

"Oh hell yeah. I've never...I don't know what this is," he

said. "Seriously, Kaelin." He rested his forehead against hers, eyes closed. "I can't stop thinking about you. I can't stop aching for you. I don't know what to do about it."

"I don't know either," she whispered. "But I know I feel the same. That's why I'm here."

He groaned again and slipped a hand beneath her legs, then stood with her in his arms. Her fingers dug into his shoulders and he strode from the living room into the short hall and into his bedroom. The blinds were still down, shutting out the evening sun, the room cool and dim. He let her feet slide to the floor, stood her in front of him and, watching her face, slowly drew the straps of her dress down her arms then pushed the bodice down to her waist. She stood before him, letting him study her, with his eyes, with his hands. He slid his hands across her shoulders, brushed over her collarbones, traced his fingertips over the curve of flesh above the edge of her hot pink lace bra.

"Very nice," he murmured, lowering his gaze to her smooth stomach. His hands slid down her sides, the inward curve of her waist, the swell of her hips, pushing the dress as he went until it slid past her hips and fell to the floor.

She tugged on his loosened tie. "This is very sexy," she murmured. "Very businesslike."

She unbuttoned his shirt and parted it to kiss his throat, her lips soft and warm. Her mouth moved lower as she unfastened each button, one by one, kiss by kiss. He started to go down, or maybe up, up in flames, especially when she reached his quivering abs and began tugging the shirt from his pants. And licked. Jesus. Christ. She licked his stomach, his bellybutton, while she opened his pants and reached inside.

He was hard, throbbing hard, and her hand closing over him sent heat racing through his veins in scorching pulses. The stroke of her hand on him had a harsh tremor shaking his body and then she went lower still, to her knees in front of him, tugging his pants down, her hands caressing his thighs. More heat rushed through his body and his brain cells started sizzling and popping. He was pretty sure that's what that noise was.

"Kaelin," he croaked, his fingers in her hair, sifting through the silky strands. And then her mouth closed over the head of his cock and he made some kind of unintelligible, embarrassing noise that almost sounded like a sob.

Scorching wet heat surrounded him, her little tongue rubbing and teasing, her mouth sucking and sliding on him. More noises escaped him, his fingers tightened in her hair. Electric thrills raced from his balls up his spine and he clenched his teeth to try to stop the whimpers in his throat. He looked down at her, her slender nose nearly pressing into his hair there, her eyes closed, her mouth stretched over his girth. Christ she could take him deep. Not all the way, because he was big and she was small, but damn, he was in her throat and she was sucking hungrily on him and making little pleasure noises.

"Damn, that's good." He managed to articulate three words. Tried for more. "So good, sweet baby. So, so good. Suck me. Oh yeah."

She opened her eyes and looked up at him, their gazes snagging and holding, her big brown eyes surrounded by long eyelashes, her cheeks pink. He caressed her cheek with his fingertips, then widened his stance and rolled his pelvis forward in a gentle thrusting motion into her mouth. Her eyes went dark and she let him fuck her mouth. Emotion punched him in the gut, took his breath away, pleasure consumed him, love and lust twisted up inside him. And then she let him slide out of her mouth and with her hand she held his cock up and dipped her head to lick his balls.

He groaned. He was dying and she was taking him down with every flick of her tongue and murmur of appreciation. Heat stabbed at him, his seed boiled in his balls and flames licked over his entire body, centered right there at her little tongue on his testicles. Holy, holy hell.

He grabbed at her hair, tried to pull her head away. "No," he groaned, though it took everything he had to try to make her stop, so close, so close. Fuck. "Not like this, Kaelin, I want..."

She pulled back and smiled up at him, the sexiest, most seductive smile he'd ever seen. "What? You only have it in you to do this once tonight?"

Damn her.

"Yes," he growled, and hauled her to her feet. Her lips were shiny and swollen and his body pulsed with urgent need. He kicked his pants and underwear aside, shucked his socks and then stripped her out of her bra and matching panties, sweet Jesus, a tiny hot pink lace triangle held together with a couple of satin ribbons. "Love your underwear, babe," he muttered, tossing them aside. Her low laugh tugged at his heart.

He fell with her onto his unmade bed, the black sheets and black and gray duvet still tangled from his restless sleep the night before, and tucked her under him, hands fisted in her long hair, holding her head while he kissed her, over and over, pressed her into the mattress, rolling his hips against hers, his cock hard and thick between them. If he didn't get inside her soon, he was going to regret not staying in her mouth, because he was starting to think if she laid a finger on him he was going to come all over her. He wanted to be inside her, and then regret crashed over him as he realized he needed a condom. He could have cried, and actually stopped kissing her to rest his forehead on hers and gasp for air, fighting for a last vestige of control.

"What?"

"Condom."

"Oh." She sounded like she might cry too.

"Got one. S'okay, baby. Just need...a...sec..." When he thought he'd gotten the throbbing, so close to the surface, so dangerously close, reduced just a bit, he rolled off her and off the bed. Top drawer, he scrabbled in there among a lot of accumulated junk, found them and ripped one open on his way back to the bed. She watched him with glowing eyes and parted lips, watched him sheathe his aching cock with trembling fingers.

Then he fell back onto her, covered her body with his and kissed her face, everywhere, her mouth, her cheek, her eyebrow, her temple. He inhaled the scent of her, that honeysuckle and apple scent he'd never forget after just one weekend, wanted to inhale all of her, to take her inside him and just hold her there forever.

"Kaelin. Kaelin. I need you."

"I know. I need you too." Her hands wandered up and down his back, pulling him close as they kissed again, as he sucked on her tongue, nipped at her lips. Heat and pressure built inside him.

He went to his knees, spread wide, found her soft center, so wet and hot, and pushed inside her in a dizzying surge. He held her waist, his hands big on her small body, as he rocked into her deeper, deeper, pleasure rolling over him in hot waves. He looked down at her lying there, so much more beautiful than she'd been at nineteen, that summer, a woman now who'd had time to learn what she wanted from life, or maybe she was just now figuring it out, and he wanted to give it to her, all of it, everything. He'd never felt like this before.

He moved over her, still rolling his hips against her in a slow surge-and-drag rhythm, took his weight on his elbows and slid his hands into her hair, pressing his face to hers, whispering her name. She held on to his shoulders and lifted into him, meeting each stroke, her soft whimpers in his ear. It was intoxicating, crazy and sexy and burning hot, as he moved in her, giving it all to her, everything he had. For the first time in his life, he wanted to say the words, wanted to tell her how he felt, but it was too soon, and he was still too afraid, still so afraid that if he said it he wouldn't hear it in return.

But he could show her his feelings, he could tell her how good it was, how sweet she was, he could make her feel so good, and he rose back to his knees and found her clit with his thumb as tingles and pressure built inside him higher and hotter. She gasped his name, and he loved the sound of it, loved how she responded to him, loved the look on her face, dazed and shattered as she came, rippling around his cock, setting off his orgasm too, his shuddering, gasping, mind-melting orgasm. He fell over her again, buried his face in her hair, breathed her in with hard gasps, pulsed inside her in aching bursts of pleasure.

After a long time, a long languorous spell of twined limbs, open-mouthed kisses, slow caresses, they lay side by side, heads on pillows, looking at each other.

"Tell me," she whispered, touching his mouth with her fingertips.

"I was afraid," he said, clasping her hand and holding it, kissing her fingers. "All my life. I told you what it was like. I know I didn't do myself any favors. I know I didn't make it easy. But I was afraid that even if I did, even if I tried to tell them the truth, it still wouldn't be good enough. Nobody would care."

"Tyler." Her soft brown eyes filled with warmth and what

looked like...love. He swallowed.

"You were too good for me," he continued. "Too nice. I was a jerk. And I kept proving it over and over again."

"You knew how I was feeling about you."

"I suspected. But I knew it could never happen. For so many reasons. I'm sorry, Kaelin. You have no idea how sorry I am."

She nodded.

"When you told my parents that you'd been there that night and stood up for me and Nick..." He closed his eyes, pressed her fingers to his mouth. "I damn near had a heart attack. I was so mad at you for doing that. And then you told them about spending the night with us. Kaelin, you didn't have to do that. Especially for me."

"Yes. I did."

"I was angry," he said quietly. "I didn't react very well. I just didn't think you should have sacrificed yourself for a jerk like me."

"Tyler, please. I don't want to hear you say that one more time. You're not a jerk. You're not."

"If you keep telling me enough, I might start believing it." He smiled at her and got a smile in return. She brushed her fingers through his hair.

"Okay. I will keep telling you. But I'm also going to tell you when you *are* acting like a jerk."

"Oh man." And there it was. All his life he'd acted like a jerk to push people away and she and Nick were the only people in the world who wouldn't let him get away with that. Somehow she'd gotten inside him, where he never let anyone get. He wrapped his arms around her and pulled her against him. She snuggled into him so warmly, so perfectly, and once more they just lay like that, wrapped in comfort and bliss.

The sound of the apartment door opening and closing caught his ear. Quiet footsteps approached down the hall. Nick. The bedroom door was open and Tyler dragged open heavy eyelids and smoothed his palm over Kaelin's butt.

Nick paused at the open door to glance in, and stopped. His eyes widened at seeing Kaelin in bed with him. He stared. Tyler started to smile, but something in Nick's expression had his gut tightening. The moment stretched out, Nick's eyebrows drawing down, his mouth thinning. "Sorry," he said quietly. He reached for the door and closed it with a soft snick, leaving Tyler and Kaelin alone.

She stirred against him half asleep and made a noise.

Tyler closed his eyes, the pain he'd seen in Nick's face like a knife twisting in his back.

Chapter Sixteen

Kaelin barely heard the door close but she felt Tyler go rigid against her. She opened sleepy eyes to look at him. "What's wrong?"

"Shit."

She shoved her hair out of her face to lift up and look at him. "Tyler? What?"

"Nick's home."

"Oh." A feeling of pleasure filled her. She'd missed Nick that week too, had longed to see him, to talk to him more. She tried to sit up. "Where'd he go?"

"I don't know."

She frowned at him. "Is everything okay?"

"I don't know."

He was closing off again, not meeting her eyes, not saying much. "Tyler. Talk to me. What is going on?"

"I think Nick might've been...surprised to see you here."

"Well, yeah."

"He didn't look happy about it."

"Oh." A pang of disappointment stirred in her. She wasn't sure how to take that, what to say. She just looked at Tyler with her questions in her eyes.

"He saw us together. He knows...he's always known how I feel about you."

"Oh." Ooooh. Things started coming together in her head. Nick telling her that he loved Tyler. This time the word came out on a sigh. "Oh." She met Tyler's eyes. "He loves you."

Tyler turned away from her, eyes closed again. "Fuck."

"Tyler." She grabbed his jaw, turned his head back. "Talk to me."

"I don't know what's going on in his head," he growled.

"Maybe we should ask him."

"You're really gonna be a pain in my ass, aren't you?" But the wry smile and the warmth in his eyes when he said it reassured her that he wasn't really angry.

She smiled. "Yeah."

"Maybe I need to figure out what's going on in my head, first," he muttered.

She blew out a soft breath. "And maybe I do too."

He looked into her eyes. "Kaelin?"

She shrugged. She was bugging him to talk about his feelings, to talk to her and to Nick, to find out what Nick was thinking, but she was just as confused. She'd come to Chicago to see both of them. The whole drive there, she'd been thinking about Tyler, yeah, but about Nick too. She'd gotten past the shame of it, the shame of wanting two men, last weekend when she'd slept with both of them at the same time, she supposed. But now, uncertainty filled her. Nick had told her he wanted her too, even though he'd also told her he loved Tyler. For some reason, coming there to see them, while scary, had seemed like the right thing to do, but now she wondered if she'd only created an even more snarled up tangle of weirdness.

"Nick and I have always...had this thing, you know," Tyler

said.

"Yes." She nodded, remembering their conversation last weekend in their hotel room.

"I always thought Nick felt different for me than I did for him."

"He loves you," she whispered.

He closed his eyes and nodded, his mouth tight.

"But you don't love him?"

His lips tightened and he looked at her with anguished eyes. A frown tugged at her eyebrows. Her stomach tensed.

"He's my friend," Tyler continued, his voice a low rasp. "But more than a friend."

"Yes." She knew that. She studied his face, could see he was trying to figure it out even as he tried to explain it to her.

"But I always figured one day maybe I'd meet someone...a woman, you know. Get married, have kids. That's how I see my life."

She swallowed through a tight, dry throat and nodded.

"I don't think Nick sees his life like that," he said, the words sounding dragged out of him. "And now, when I'm kind of feeling like maybe I have met that woman..."

Her heart stuttered in her chest then raced crazily as he held her gaze.

"I have this crazy sick feeling in my gut. Because...dammit..." He closed his eyes again, his mouth a hard line in his face. "I care about him. He's stuck with me through everything. He doesn't take any shit from me. And he loves me anyway. And I don't want to lose him." His eyes opened, and she saw the realization there. "Fuck. I do love him."

She nodded, her mind spinning, her heart thudding

painfully.

"That's not something every woman would get," Tyler continued, reaching out to touch her cheek. "It's not something every woman would put up with. Or could handle."

What was he saying? Was he asking her to handle it? Was he saying he wanted them both in his life?

She took a breath. "There's something you should know."

He lifted his eyebrows.

"Ever since you and Nick left Mapleglen, he and I have sort of kept in touch."

His eyebrows pulled down. "What do you mean 'sort of kept in touch'?"

She bit her lip briefly. "We've emailed back and forth a few times. Not a lot. Just keeping in touch."

His frown deepened. "Why?"

She stroked a finger over one thick, gold eyebrow, then stroked her fingers through his silky hair. "Because he's a friend. I...I've always liked Nick." Her stomach tightened and she swallowed. "I came here to see you, but I came to see him too. After that night, I'm having just as hard a time as you figuring this all out. I care about Nick too."

He stared at her. Then he said, "Why didn't Nick tell me that?"

"That we'd kept in touch? Because I asked him not to."

Tyler sat there for a moment then said, "I should be pissed at him for that. But damn. He's a good guy."

"Yes. He is." She held his gaze. "I know he...he said he wanted me. That night. And I know he loves you. But I guess I don't really know how he feels about me. This. Us." She waved a hand. "It's kind of crazy."

His eyelids drooped, his lips pursed. "Yeah," he said heavily. "It is. I know."

"D'you think Nick would go for it?"

His eyes flew open again. He stared at her searchingly. "Are *you* willing to go for it?"

She smiled and nodded.

"Then I guess we'd better ask him." He smiled as he repeated her words. "Just so you know, we haven't been getting along that great this week. He's pissed at me, and I can only think that it's because of how I treated you."

She nodded, her breath coming in choppy bursts, her heart pattering.

Tyler threw back the covers and swung his long legs off the bed. He reached for a pair of jeans hanging over a chair and stepped into them. She sat on the side of the bed, watching him. Despite her confusion and anxiety, it was impossible not be affected by the sight of his beautiful body, his thighs strong as he stood on one leg, then the other, his soft penis still impressive and beautiful in its thick nest of dark gold curls, his long muscles rippling under golden skin as he zipped up, the jeans riding low on his lean hips.

He held out a hand to her and she rose, looked around for something to put on. She grabbed the gray dress shirt she'd peeled Tyler out of earlier and pushed her arms into it. On her, it was voluminous and she fastened only a couple of buttons with shaky fingers, rolled up the sleeves then took Tyler's hand. She followed him out of the bedroom. He turned left in the hall and took a few long steps to the door just down the hall—Nick's bedroom?

He knocked on the closed door but didn't wait to be invited to enter, just opened the door and walked in, pulling Kaelin along behind him. Her tummy felt quivery, her lungs tight.

212

"Hey," Tyler said. Nick leaned against the wall, standing in front of the window, his room overlooking the street out front. His head snapped around as they walked in. He straightened.

"What's up?" he asked, shoving his hands in his jeans pockets. "Hey, Kaelin." He smiled at her and she gave him a shaky smile back. He lifted one eyebrow. "Didn't know you were coming."

"Neither did I," she confessed, and his smile went crooked.

"You okay?"

"Mmmm. Maybe."

He lowered his chin, cast a glance at Tyler.

"We need to talk, buddy," Tyler said. "This isn't going to be easy."

Nick held up a hand. "Hey. No worries. I could see you two worked things out, I guess. I'm glad." He nodded.

"Yeah." Tyler pulled Kaelin further into the room, tucked her into his arms in front of him. "I'm not sure if we've worked things out. Not everything. We talked. I apologized."

Nick nodded slowly. "Good."

"The thing is..." Tyler's voice cracked. He lifted a hand to rub his face and Kaelin peeked over her shoulder at him. Her heart full and aching for both of them, she only wanted to make things right for them. Tension thickened around them, and Nick's throat worked as he swallowed.

"I said, no worries." Nick gave them a thin smile. "You don't need to explain it to me, man." His expression gentled. "I've always known how you felt about Kaelin. I've always known how she felt about you. If anything good came out of that screwed-up family wedding, it's you two being together. I'm happy for you."

Tyler gave a short laugh. "Yeah, you are so right about

that." He paused. "But..."

Nick turned away then, and moved to the old oak dresser in the corner. "So," he said, his back toward them. "What's gonna happen? Kaelin, you moving to Chicago?"

"We haven't thought that far ahead." With another glance at Tyler over her shoulder, she released herself from his arms and moved toward Nick. She touched his back. He didn't turn, just bent his head. "Nick." She rubbed up and down. "Oh, Nick."

"Don't fucking feel sorry for me," he said in a low, tight voice, head still down. "I'm fine."

"I know. I don't feel sorry for you." She spoke in a low voice too. "Nick. I know you love him. I think I-I love him too." Her nerves stretched like rubber bands, she willed her shaky voice to be steady. "But I also care about you."

He nodded stiffly. "Kaelin. You know I care about you too."

Tyler moved up to them then, to stand behind Nick. He slid his arms around Nick and rested his head against Nick's. Nick went very still, his fingers gripping the edge of the dresser, still looking down at it.

"What you said that day," Tyler said. "When we were in Mapleglen and you said it was insulting to you that I thought Kaelin was too good for me, but you weren't...I've been thinking about that." Tyler paused. "You probably are too good for me. And I want you to know how much that means to me that you care about me. Nick. I've never told you this." His voice came out thick. "I don't want to lose you."

"What are you saying?" Nick asked after a long moment of dense silence.

"He's saying, *we* don't want to lose you," Kaelin said. She rested her hand on his taut forearm. "I'm confused, too, Nick. This is the weirdest thing that's ever happened to me. I want two men. Me. The good girl. I don't know what happened to me last weekend, but for some reason this just all feels like this is the way it should be. The three of us. "

Nick groaned and still didn't move. Tyler's hand rubbed over his chest. "Jesus," Nick said. He turned his head and met Kaelin's eyes. "Are you sure, Kaelin? A lot of people would think that's really fucked up."

"I know." She smiled and held his gaze. "I'm sure. You know I've always cared about you. You were always a friend to me. Last weekend...well, it was more than just friends. Right?" She bit her lip as she awaited his answer.

"You know it was, honey." He released his grip on the dresser and found her hand with his. His big warm fingers closed around hers. "You know it was."

He turned in Tyler's arms to face his friend. "Tyler. Buddy. What the fuck?"

Tyler gave a choked laugh. "Yeah. What the fuck is right. I don't know, man. You think I can explain any of this? All I know is what I want. I want you. And I want Kaelin. And I think..." He paused, glanced at Kaelin, wrapped one arm around her shoulders, the other around Nick's, pulled their three heads close together. "I think we are so fucking lucky to have found her, probably the only woman in the world who'd get this."

She huffed out a little laugh, pleasure sliding through her at his words. "I don't know about that," she said. "I can't be the only woman in the world who'd fall in love with both of you. I saw the girls who chased you both in high school. I'm kinda thinking I'm the lucky one, here, the one who has two guys who care about me. That's...unbelievable."

Nick's arm came around her too, and she realized he'd put the other arm around Tyler and they stood in a circle, holding each other.

"I guess we're all the lucky ones," Tyler said. "Probably me most of all. I never felt like I was worth loving by anyone. And now I have both of you." His voice choked up and he squeezed his eyes closed. Kaelin's throat tightened up too, and for long moments they just held each other.

Tyler lifted his head and his mouth met hers in a hard, fierce kiss. He turned to Nick and kissed him too, his arm around Nick's neck. Then he looked him in the eyes. "I love you, Nick." Nick's eyes closed, his Adam's apple bobbed, his mouth compressed, and then they kissed again. Emotion swelled in Kaelin's chest watching them.

The kiss escalated into scorching, and Tyler moved back and forth between Nick and Kaelin, nipping at lips, licking inside their mouths, and then Kaelin turned to Nick and kissed him too, so hot and heartfelt, and when they broke apart, breathing heavy, she looked at Tyler and the look in his eyes almost took her knees out, the hottest, most profound worship and love she'd ever seen.

"Come back to bed," Tyler murmured. "Both of you." And he took both their hands and led them from Nick's room, with a smaller double bed, to his with its massive king-size bed.

Kaelin wanted this to be about Nick. She and Tyler had had their moments earlier and this had to be for Nick, and when she and Tyler exchanged glances she knew he felt the same.

"Wanna fuck you," Tyler whispered against Nick's mouth as he undid Nick's jeans.

Nick groaned and their kisses went hard, savage. They each shoved off their jeans, and Nick broke the kiss long enough to yank his T-shirt over his head. Kaelin took it from his hands and tossed it onto the chair, stroked her hands down their backs as they kissed again, now naked, their hard, muscled bodies pressed together, their hands fisted in each other's hair.

They moved to the bed and Tyler pushed Nick down on his back. Nick went to roll over, and Tyler stopped him. "Face to face," he growled. Nick adjusted his position on the bed and held out a hand to Kaelin. She smiled, her chest feeling so full and tight, and sat beside him on the bed, rubbed his chest. He sucked in air, as Tyler moved over him and kissed him again.

Tyler lifted up to kiss Kaelin once more, with a lingering stroke of his tongue over her bottom lip, and a heated eye-lock that seared her soul, before he started kissing his way down Nick's body. She watched, heat rolling over her body in hot, erotic waves, as Tyler licked Nick's nipples, kissed his rippled abs, shifted lower and...and... She let out the breath she hadn't realized she'd been holding when Tyler took Nick's cock in his mouth.

Her body turned to liquid as she watched, wide-eyed, aching inside with an intense need, mesmerized by their passion for each other. Nick reached for her hand and clasped it, and her heart swelled. She looked at his face, saw his eyes close in ecstasy, his mouth open. She leaned over and brushed a kiss on his lips, then licked her own lips. Watching with avid eyes as Tyler closed his mouth over Nick's cock and slid down it, then back up, sucking.

Ohgodohgodohgod, that was so hot, so hot, so hot. She pressed a hand between her legs where she ached.

Tyler sucked on him, licked him, rubbed the head of Nick's cock around his lips and sucked him again, Nick's cock filling his mouth. Then he moved lower still, pushed Nick's legs up, so he could nuzzle Nick's balls, and lick and suck there.

Nick groaned, his fingers tightened on hers and Kaelin's bare, wet pussy pulsed against her own palm. Oh god.

"Kaelin."

Her eyes flew to Tyler's face.

"Can you reach into that drawer there and find the bottle of lube?"

She quickly stretched out and yanked open the drawer, found the bottle and handed it to Tyler. He squeezed some of the liquid into his palm, drizzled more all over Nick's cock and balls, and then he rubbed it in, making both their cocks all slick and shiny, long and hard, roped with heavy veins, and Kaelin thought she was going to die from the excitement of watching this. Her heart fluttered in a fast, uneven rhythm, her breath coming in short pants.

Nick groaned again and released her hand to slide his hands beneath his knees, pulling them back toward his chest. His cock pulsed on his belly as Tyler moved between his legs, on his knees, his cock in his hand, and when Tyler pushed into him, Nick's face contorted and he gave a softy cry.

"Oh yeah," Tyler said. "Gonna fuck you now. Gonna fuck you so hard."

"Yes. Do it."

Kaelin's eyes widened as she watched, her breath quickening even more. Tyler hadn't used a condom, was bare inside Nick, but they'd been together a long time and had probably had that conversation, and she trusted they'd be having that conversation with her soon.

Acting on instinct, she reached for Nick's cock, all slicked up with lube, and stroked him.

"Oh yeah," Nick said. He turned his face into the pillow. "Oh Christ, that's good, yeah, Kaelin, honey."

She met Tyler's eyes, blazing cobalt blue, returned her gaze to Nick's beautiful cock and balls, and to where their bodies joined so intimately. More waves of heat swept over her as she pulled on Nick's shaft, hand sliding easily, then faster as Tyler moved faster against him, inside him, harder, faster, slamming into him.

The sound of their bodies slapping, Nick's muted noises, and Tyler's deep groans of pleasure filled the room. So beautiful, so hot, so moving. Something she never in her craziest fantasies would have imagined, but she was there, loving them, both of them, and it was right and perfect.

Tyler held Nick's legs, his chest and six-pack abs gleaming with perspiration, his face tight and intense, and he pounded into him. Kaelin licked her lips, gripped Nick's cock tighter. Her pussy tightened and pulsed, so close to coming and she wasn't even touching herself. She concentrated on Nick, on the cadence of her hand on him, moving faster.

"Gonna come," he muttered thickly, head moving on the pillow. "Fuck me, I'm gonna...ungh." His words turned in to a growl and he pulsed in her hand, so alive, so hot, white jets of semen spurting onto his belly. She watched with fascination and then Tyler shouted, too, holding himself against Nick's body, eyes closed, fingers gripping Nick's legs.

She had to come too, had to, and she slipped her hand between her legs and rubbed furiously, so aroused it only took seconds before she did. When she opened her eyes, both guys watched her, with heavy-lidded, hot eyes. "Aw, sweet baby," Tyler rasped. "So hot, baby."

They all collapsed together on the bed. After a few long moments of sucked-in breaths, Tyler moved and drew up the tangled covers, Kaelin in the middle. And they all slept.

They awoke late in the morning, blinds blocking out most of the sun but not all, but this time there was no panic, no fleeing from the room. Other than Tyler, who, after lying there for a few minutes, flung back the covers and leaped out of bed.

"I can't lie around all day," he declared.

Nick lifted a head and gave him a bleary-eyed gaze. "Then make yourself useful and make some coffee for us."

Tyler disappeared out of the room and Nick pulled Kaelin in against his body. "He's a morning person. I got no problem lying around in bed," he muttered in her ear.

She laughed softly and snuggled into him. "Me neither."

They kissed, just the two of them, long, open-mouthed kisses, Nick's hand sliding up and down her back, while she got hotter and he got harder.

When Tyler returned with three cups of coffee, they turned to him, Kaelin in a haze of lust. "Oh," she mumbled. "Oh yeah. Coffee."

Tyler snorted and set the mugs on the table beside the bed. "Apparently you forgot all about it. And me."

She shot him a gaze, but recognized the teasing glint in his eye, and she held out a hand to him. He slid back into bed, pressing her between their bodies. Nick continued kissing her mouth, her cheek, her jaw, while Tyler's lips nibbled at the sensitive nape of her neck and his tongue dragged over her shoulder.

They played like that for a long time, exploring each other's bodies, tasting and teasing, petting and pleasing, heat building, sweetness expanding. Kaelin had never felt so adored, so worshiped as they touched her and whispered to her. It was intoxicating, dizzying, gratifying. She took pleasure too, in touching them, threading her fingers through silky hair, brushing over taut nipples, filling her hand with thick columns of throbbing flesh.

Then Nick flipped to his back, bringing her on top of him,

their mouths fused in a lush kiss. "Mmm, nice," she murmured against his lips and wriggled her body. He groaned, and then she felt Tyler behind her, stroking her butt, finding Nick's cock. He must've grabbed a condom. She bit her lip. Damn. She really didn't want them to use it, wanted to feel them bare inside her, but for now, better safe than sorry. Wasn't that always her motto?

Tyler rolled the condom onto Nick's cock, and then helped him find his way inside Kaelin in a stretching push into her. He filled her so beautifully and she moved on top of him, rising to ride him.

Nick watched her with hot eyes, his gaze dropping to her breasts. "So beautiful," he murmured. He reached for them, filled his hands with them then pinched her nipples, sensation cascading from nipple to womb. She moved on top of him, up and down, Tyler's hand on her back then gathering her hair at her nape. Then he pushed her down, back down to lay on Nick's chest, with a gentle pressure on her back. She kissed Nick and rubbed her face against his.

Delicious. So hot and sexy and delicious.

"You are beautiful, Kaelin," Tyler whispered from behind her. His hand on her butt made her twitch. His fingers teased her anus, sending sparks cascading outward over her body from there, making her pussy tighten so much around Nick's cock that he groaned. He pressed her face to his neck again, thrusting up into her while Tyler played with her ass, teasing and stroking and then probing lightly, so gently. She whimpered again. She'd never done this, wasn't sure if she wanted to do it, but, helpless to the fiery pleasure torching her entire body, she let it continue.

"So pretty there," Tyler whispered. "So damn tight and pretty." When his finger breached her, sharp sensation stabbed then retreated and she let out the breath she'd been holding.

"Need lube," Tyler muttered and his finger withdrew and the bed shifted as he moved. Nick continued slowly fucking up into her, arms around her, holding her so tightly, reassuringly. She heard the noises of Tyler opening a bottle, a squirting sound and then felt the coolness as his lubed-up fingers slicked over her ass again. This time his penetration didn't startle her as much, and when he moved his finger inside her and stroked over nerve endings there, her head lifted in shock. Fiery ecstasy tore through her body and she cried out.

Oh sweet Jesus, that felt incredible! She never, ever would have thought that sensation there, combined with her pussy being filled, would create such a wild and violent pleasure. Everything inside her tightened and drew up in a tight, hard point of nearly painful ecstasy. She was going to come, already, too fast. She didn't want this to end already.

As if sensing that, Tyler withdrew from her. He moved over her, straddling both her and Nick, his cock warm and heavy on her lower back as he kissed her shoulder, supporting his weight on his arms. "Wanna fuck you there," he murmured into her ear. "So Nick and I are both fucking you at the same time."

She knew it was a question and that he was waiting for a response. If she wanted him to stop, he would. She should stop him. But she couldn't say no. But she couldn't quite say yes, either.

Tyler scooped her hair off her face and held it with one hand. "Kaelin. I won't do it unless you say yes. Unless you say you want it."

Oh god, he was going to make her do it. She knew exactly why, last weekend, she'd wanted to be restrained, wanted that responsibility taken away from her. But that Tyler knew and understood...knew how she'd never been able to express what

One Wicked Night

she wanted, how most of her life what she'd wanted hadn't mattered. He understood. Even though she wanted him to just do it, it meant so much that he wouldn't do this without her consent. She liked that.

"Yes," she hissed. "Damn you, yes. That's what I want."

She was sandwiched between them, her body a hot glow of pleasure. Tyler took a moment for more lube, and she pictured him rolling a condom on his cock, all thick and shiny and ribbed with veins. Then the blunt head was nudging her entrance. She squeezed her eyes closed.

"Relax, Kaelin," Nick soothed again, stroking her back, holding her head. "Relax. It'll be so good, sweetheart."

Tyler eased into her slowly, so slowly and carefully, and again his thoughtful patience warmed her inside. But despite his care, he was huge and she was untried there, and a sharp burst of fiery pain flashed over her. Oh god, he was splitting her ass in two! She cried out, bit her lip hard to stifle another cry. Nick continued to whisper soft words in her ear and stroke her back and neck.

"Ah, Kaelin." Tyler's voice was hoarse. "I'm sorry, babe, I know at first it hurts...stay with me. Bear down. Like you're pushing me out."

"I want to do it," she whispered. "I want to." She wanted to do it for them. She tried to control her trembling body and do as he said and miraculously he eased farther into her. The pain shifted into hot ecstasy, washing over her in waves of heat, a burning rapture. Oh dear god.

So full. So incredibly full, Nick's cock in her pussy stroking, stroking, deep inside her, sliding over nerve endings, Tyler's cock in her ass touching forbidden sensitive places inside her there. Her head whirled at the eroticism of it. It was her darkest, wildest fantasy come true, both of them like this.

223

She let herself slip into near delirium, floating on white-hot pleasure, fire rippling under her skin, heating her up. She moaned again and again, unable to stop the noises that escaped her.

"Fuck, that feels good," Tyler groaned, and he bent over her and dragged his tongue over her back, kissed her shoulder. "So good, babe. So hot and tight."

"Can you feel each other?" She managed to put words together into a question.

"Yeah." Tyler nuzzled her hair then rose up again. "Yeah, I can feel his dick inside your pussy."

They found a rhythm and moved together, rocking into her in seductive, sensuous slides, and that coil of heat inside her twisted and tightened again, building, higher, higher. It kept building so high it almost scared her, she'd never been that high before, reaching for that incredible sharp point of almost painful ecstasy. The pressure of Tyler's damp body from behind and Nick's body on her clit gave her the final stimulation she needed to send her flying. Sparks exploded in front of her eyes, fire raced through her veins and she lost all awareness of what was happening, other than the feelings rocketing through her body.

Only vague awareness teased the edges of her consciousness when Nick and Tyler came too, shouting and groaning their own pleasure, pulsing inside her in heavy jerks, pressing their bodies so tightly to her, squeezing her between them, the three of them joined like that in an incredible, intimate connection. The completion of it, the perfect grace and beauty and generosity of it, touched her soul. Her heart turned over in her chest and she knew she was utterly lost, all of her, her body, her heart, her soul, lost to them—both of them.

Chapter Seventeen

"Damn. Coffee's cold." Nick put on a pout.

Kaelin huffed out a laugh and snuggled under the covers.

"You can't stay in bed all day," Tyler said. After that powerful, draining orgasm, he'd crashed again in a short nap, but now felt full of energy, practically vibrating with it. "Come on, get up. I'll make more coffee."

Kaelin opened one eye to peek at Nick, who met her gaze and smiled lazily.

Tyler watched them, a hot softness expanding in his chest. There were going to be some growing pains as they all learned about each other and figured things out. But he could handle it.

With an exaggerated stretch and yawn, Kaelin got out of bed. "Damn," she said. "My bag is still in my car. I don't have anything to wear."

"You looked good in that shirt of mine," Tyler said with a wicked grin.

"Better than good," Nick added, patting her naked butt as he walked past her.

She grabbed his shirt again and slipped it on, this time finding her panties too. She followed him to their small kitchen where he started making coffee, and climbed up onto a stool at the counter.

"How long can you stay?" he asked, pouring the dregs of the last pot into the sink.

"Well. I'm on vacation for two weeks, but I can't leave Taz for very long."

"Is he home alone?" Tyler frowned, his hand pausing with a scoop of coffee in it.

"No! Of course not! He's having sleepovers at the neighbors'."

"Ah."

"I miss him," she said, looking down, and his heart tightened a little.

"We can have pets here," he said casually.

Her eyes brightened. "Really?"

He nodded, chest tightening a little more. "Yeah. Cats and small dogs. And you know what else?"

"What?"

"Some of the best law schools in the country are here in Chicago."

"That is true." They shared a long, smiling moment.

"Are you hungry?"

"Yeah." She tipped her head to one side. "I feel like pancakes."

He shot her an amused glance. "Really."

Her saucy smile tightened his heart in his chest and he reached out to cup her cheek with gentle reverence. Christ. How the hell had he gotten so lucky?

The knock on the apartment door made them both jump. Their eyes met in a silent question. Tyler shrugged, but headed to the door, wearing only his unbuttoned jeans, but Nick beat him there, dressed in a pair of shorts he'd retrieved from his own room. The door opened to reveal—

"Mom."

Feeling as if the air had been sucked out of his lungs, Tyler stared at his mother.

Her smile was uncertain, hesitant, tremulous. "Hi, Tyler."

He frowned, standing there just behind Nick. "What are you doing here?"

"I need to talk to you. I'm sorry to barge in. I'm on my way to the airport."

"Airport? Where are you going? And where's Dad?"

"He's at home." Sadness dimmed her smile. "I'm on my way to Italy."

"Italy! Jesus Christ." He gaped at her then shoved a hand in his hair. "Uh. Well. Come in." And then he remembered Kaelin sitting at the counter separating living room from small kitchen, wearing only his shirt with one button done up and a tiny pair of panties.

Mom saw her at that moment, too, stopped and went very still. "Kaelin."

Kaelin's eyes shifted from one person to the other and back again but she put on a brave smile. "Hi, Mrs. Wirth."

Mom walked farther into the living room, clutching her purse to her. "I didn't expect to see you here." Then she smiled, warmly, genuinely. "But I'm happy to see you here."

Huh? There wasn't much doubt about what was going on, given Kaelin's skimpy attire and his own half-dressed state, and what she made of Nick being in on all this, he had no idea. His mind was still reeling from seeing her there.

"I'm just making coffee," he told his mom, freaked out at how normal and polite and host-like his comment was. "Want some?"

"Yes. That would be nice."

His chest clenched as he poured fresh coffee into mugs. Sticky silence hovered around them.

"So. What's going on?" he asked his mom.

She smiled, looking strangely more at ease now she'd seen Kaelin there.

"Well. Like I said, I'm on my way to Italy."

"Why?"

"I've always wanted to go there. I'm going on a cooking holiday. I'll be staying in a little apartment and taking cooking lessons, and touring olive groves and wineries."

"Uh. Wow." She'd always liked to cook, but…wow.

She looked down at her coffee, then back up. "I've been trying to convince your father to travel with me, maybe even retire, but he's not interested in that. So I've decided to go myself." She bit her lip briefly.

"Mom. Are you and Dad splitting up?" A rock materialized in Tyler's gut.

"Well. Not exactly. But I think some time apart will be good for us." Her eyelashes drifted down. "I haven't been entirely happy for some time and I think we need to do this. Figure things out. Last weekend was…difficult. But in a way, it finally got some things out in the open that needed to be said." She looked at up him sadly. "I just wanted to keep our family together."

"Jesus, Mom."

"I still love him," she said. "I just need to figure out what I want my life to be. You know, when you've been married thirty years you start to take things for granted. Maybe some time apart will help that."

Tyler had a feeling there was a lot more to it than that. He appreciated that his mom wasn't there bad-mouthing his dad or blaming him for whatever had happened, but he sensed her unhappiness with his dad, remembering last weekend, when he'd tried to talk to them, the tension between them, remembering how for the first time in his life they hadn't been a united front against him.

"But that's not really why I'm here," Mom said. "Well, I wanted you to know that, but mostly I wanted to apologize." She sighed and lifted her cup to her lips. After taking a sip, she continued. "I'm so sorry about last weekend. I'm so sorry about...everything." She lifted her blue eyes to meet his. "I'm sorrier than you'll ever know that you thought I believed you would rape someone. Truly, Tyler, I never really believed it."

"Then why did you kick me out?" he said, disturbed at how low and shaky his voice was.

"It was still an incredibly stupid thing to do," she admonished him. "Putting yourself in that position. Clearly *something* happened that night. Even though I believed you never forced that girl into anything, it was mortifying to have her parents contacting us and accusing you of that, and then having to give them money to keep it quiet."

"That was your choice."

"Yes." She nodded. "It was. Oh, Tyler. You were only *seventeen years old* and you were doing crazy things like that! Tying a girl up! Naked! You were getting wilder and wilder and I thought..." She paused. "It seemed like we needed to take drastic measures. It was the hardest thing I've ever done." Then she made a face. "Maybe. To this day I wonder if it was the right choice. I never imagined it would turn into ten years without seeing you." She waved a hand. "But we can't go back and change things. All I can do is tell you how sorry I am. And last weekend, yes, I know we overreacted about that rumor. I don't want to blame your father, because lord knows I haven't been without blame in this whole thing, but this time we really did have a...difference of opinion about how that was handled. I knew he was furious, and I was going to try to smooth things over but I didn't really get a chance. I really don't care if you took ten hookers up to your room." She shot an apologetic glance at Kaelin. "I don't mean you, dear."

"I know." Kaelin smiled briefly.

Mom sighed. "That's not entirely true," she said. "Hookers...well...I hope you never have to resort to that. But..." She held up a hand. "It's none of my business. But it did disturb me again that something like that happened. I could kick myself, but I did have a moment where I was annoyed at you for acting so irresponsibly."

Kaelin covered her mouth with her hand.

"But that's all it was," Mom continued. "It wasn't life or death or anything to get so worked up about."

This was freaking him out. He rubbed the back of his neck, glanced at Nick and Kaelin, who both took it all in, trying to keep their faces expressionless, apparently. Though when his eyes met Kaelin's he saw a hint of a smile.

"But most of all, I wanted to tell you how proud I am of you." Her voice caught. "I wanted to tell you last weekend. I was looking forward to you coming home, so I could finally tell you how proud I am of all that you've accomplished. Your life was spiraling out of control, and I'm so proud of what you've made of yourself. I could see how bright you were, how creative, how talented. I didn't know what you were going to end up doing..."

"Neither did I," Tyler said dryly.

She smiled, eyes shining. "But I wanted you to have the best life you could. To make the most of yourself. That's all any mother wants, I think. I just didn't do a good job of telling you that, I guess."

"Mom." His chest ached and emotions swirled inside him.

"I'm proud of you. And I love you. It hurt me to see you so angry at people who love you, just because you think you're not worthy of their love." She glanced at Kaelin, and then, surprisingly, at Nick. "But you are. And I think...I hope...maybe you're figuring that out."

Tyler didn't know what to say.

"We're trying to show him, Mrs. Wirth," Kaelin said softly.

Mom turned to Kaelin and studied her face. "And you, dear...have *you* figured things out?"

"I think so." She smiled.

Mom touched Kaelin's cheek, her smile full of warm affection. "I'm so glad, dear. I always had this feeling that you weren't entirely happy. I hated to think that you were going to end up feeling like..." She hesitated. "End up feeling unsatisfied."

"You're okay with...this?" Kaelin asked. "With us?"

"I am if you love him."

Kaelin nodded. Christ. Tyler scowled. She'd told Nick she loved him, she'd told his mom she loved him, but she still hadn't told *him*. But then, he hadn't told her yet either. Suddenly Tyler felt a little less afraid of that and some of the tension eased out of him.

Mom looked at him, fiercely. "And you. Don't hurt her. You may be too big for me to spank, but you'll hear from me if you do that. Understand?"

"Yes, Mom." Her protectiveness of Kaelin startled him, warmed him inside, but not as much as the way she stood up to him. Jesus. It really did make him feel—strangely—loved.

"I should go." She set down her cup on the counter. She

paused. "Do you think I could have a hug?"

Tyler's feet felt frozen to the ground. His throat closed up and he tried to swallow. It was hard to get past all the old hurt in just a few minutes. No, it was impossible. But the look on his mom's face, so vulnerable, so tender, wrenched at his heart, and he moved around the small counter and took her in his arms. She hugged him fiercely back.

"You will never know how much I regret the last ten years," she said, her voice clogged with tears. "How I wish I'd been smarter or stronger..."

"It's okay, Mom. I could have done things differently too." His throat tightened and he closed his eyes and hugged her. "And maybe..." It killed him to say it, but... "Maybe what you did *was* for the best. For me."

She drew back, eyes wet but a smile on her face. She nodded. "You were a child, Tyler. Don't blame yourself for how you reacted. But now, it takes a man to say something like that. You're a good man, Tyler." She patted his cheek. "Okay. I have to get to the airport."

"Are you driving? How did you get here?"

"I have my car. I've arranged long-term parking for it. I'll be in touch. I'll email you from Sabina."

"Okay. Geez, Mom. Take care of yourself. Are you sure..." The idea of his mom flying half way around the world, to a strange country, all by herself, suddenly bothered him.

"I'm sure." She turned to Kaelin and opened her arms for a hug, and Kaelin hugged her too. Then she turned to Nick and got another hug. Drawing back, she smiled up at him. "I'm not sure if I'm ready to know everything, but...I want you to be happy too, Nick."

He nodded, his silvery gray eyes shining, a bemused smile on his mouth.

When she'd left, the three of them stood there looking at each other.

"Whoa," Tyler said. He felt a little...drained. But exhilarated. Powerful. As if he could take on the world and win. He looked at Nick. "We're not taking that Healthy Solutions account."

Nick's mouth dropped open. "What?"

Tyler headed down the hall. "I'm going back to bed." He shot them both a grin over his shoulder.

Nick stomped down the hall after him. "Where the hell did that come from?" he yelled.

Tyler stripped off his jeans and jumped on the bed. "I was thinking about it yesterday."

"You're fucking nuts, man," Nick said, but he smiled and unzipped his shorts. Kaelin walked in behind him, shaking her head.

"I thought you didn't like lying around in bed all day," she said.

"I'm not planning to just lie around. C'mere, sweet baby. Nick and I want to do all kinds of wicked things to you."

She kept his shirt on and climbed up between them. "Oh yay. I like wicked things."

His chest expanded and he glanced at Nick, who smiled too.

"You know there *is* something I want you to do," Kaelin said, stretching out on the bed. "I want you to tie me up."

Tyler's dick leaped and he licked his lips. "Uh...sure, babe."

"I mean, tie me up and do wicked things to me." She held his gaze meaningfully.

He stared at her, heart thudding. "You mean..."

"Yes."

"I can't..."

"Tyler." She reached for his hand and inserted her fingers between his, curling them together. "I trust you enough to let you tie me up. Do you trust me enough to do it?"

His heart swelled up so huge he thought it might explode out of his chest and he closed his eyes against the wave of emotion washing over him. Yeah, hell yeah, he trusted her. After what she'd done for him, he trusted her with his life, and he'd always trusted Nick.

"I love you, Kaelin," he said hoarsely, giving in to his last fear. "Yes, I trust you. I trust you and love you. He looked at Nick. "Both of you."

For a guy who'd never thought he was worth being loved by anybody, now he had two people who loved him. Maybe he'd actually start believing he deserved it, wasn't sure why he was so lucky, but he was so damn grateful, and he planned to spend the rest of his life showing them that. Starting right now, giving Kaelin what she wanted.

He could do that. He could tie her up. He was into that, had always liked the control, the power. He knew the trust required for her to let herself be bound. It took even more trust for her to admit and ask for what she really wanted, putting her at her most vulnerable. He recognized the power he had over her because of that. But he also recognized the deep responsibility it gave him.

He looked at Nick, at the love and trust in his eyes, and recognized the same truth. A sense of strength and a deep desire to live up to that responsibility filled him, like water in a well, seeping into every crevice of his being.

Loving and trusting someone had always seemed to him to be the ultimate vulnerability. But now he could see that loving and trusting someone wasn't just the ultimate vulnerability—it was the ultimate strength. That in finally letting himself love and be loved, he was freeing himself from the worst kind of bondage. That the exchange between the three of them made them all vulnerable—but made them all stronger.

About the Author

Kelly Jamieson lives in Winnipeg, Canada and is the author of over twenty romance novels and novellas. Her writing has been described as "emotionally complex", "sweet and satisfying" and "blisteringly sexy". If she can stop herself from reading or writing, she loves to cook. She has shelves of cookbooks that she reads at length. She also enjoys gardening in the summer, and in the winter she likes to read gardening magazines and seed catalogues (there might be a theme here...). She also loves shopping, especially for clothes and shoes.

She loves hearing from readers, so please visit her website at KellyJamieson.com or contact her at info@kellyjamieson.com.

To find happiness, first you have to find yourself.

Lost and Found
© 2010 Kelly Jamieson

Krissa has always been the responsible one. Driven to fulfill her mother's abandoned dreams, to make her husband Derek happy. She's brought that single-minded determination to the one dream she has for herself—a child. Except she and Derek can't conceive, and Derek refuses to consider using a stranger's sperm. The result? Guilt that her desperation is causing their marital rift.

The last thing they need is a long-term houseguest, but Derek's best friend Nate, a nomadic photographer recovering from a career-threatening eye disorder, has nowhere else to go.

Nate thought his friends' home would be a temporary haven from the grief that has dogged his heels since his wife died. Instead he's in the middle of a marriage in meltdown. Soon their friendship develops an underlying hum of forbidden sexual tension. When Krissa proposes a wild idea—that Nate be their sperm donor—Derek has an even wilder proposal: bypass the fertility clinic and accept Nate's donation straight from the source.

At first, Krissa believes she's on the fast track to having her dream. But it quickly becomes clear that when the heart gets involved—and secrets are revealed—the simplest of arrangements can become entangled beyond belief. Or repair…

Warning: This title contains a man who's lost, the woman he finds, sizzling ménage sex, tender romantic sex, love lost and love found.

Available now in ebook and print from Samhain Publishing.

When you're down on the farm, things are bound to get dirty!

Carnal Compromise
© 2011 Robin L. Rotham

Joe Remke has just one qualification for his lovers—he wants them gone before sunrise, which makes his new bunkmate AJ about as safe as a woman can be around him. It also makes his determination to sleep with his boss downright stupid, because if Brent ever gives in, he'll be looking for a new job.

Ladies' man Brent Andersen knows sex with his right-hand man Joe is inevitable, but he's not going down without a fight. Putting the new female hired hand in their cramped RV was a stroke of genius, taking the heat off him while protecting her from the horny guys on his custom farming crew.

AJ Pender's hard-bodied roomies may hide their feelings for each other from the rest of the crew, but they aren't fooling her—Brent and Joe are hot for each other, and it's all she can do not to cry at the thought. If they ever found out she fantasizes about being the meat in their farmer sandwich, they'd probably die laughing.

Fortunately for Brent and Joe, fantasies have a way of revealing themselves and AJ's are right up their alley. But even threesomes have their risks, and AJ can serve as a buffer for only so long before the tension between them explodes.

Warning: Flying BOBs ahead—and that's just the warm-up! Strap yourself in for a wild ride complete with ménage, m/m, and a voyeuristic f/f scene hot enough to make three grown men beg for mercy.

Available now in ebook and print from Samhain Publishing.

www.samhainpublishing.com

Green for the planet.
Great for your wallet.

It's all about the story...

Romance

HORROR

Retro ROMANCE

www.samhainpublishing.com